ONLY AN ALLIGATOR

Also by Steve Aylett

Slaughtermatic
The Crime Studio
Bigot Hall
Toxicology
The Inflatable Volunteer
Atom

ONLY AN ALLIGATOR

STEVE AYLETT

GOLLANCZ
London

This edition first published in Great Britain in 2001 by

Gollancz
An imprint of the Orion Publishing Group
Orion House, 5 Upper St Martin's Lane,
London WC2H 9EA

A CIP catalogue record for this book
is available from the British Library

ISBN 0 575 069066

Typeset at The Spartan Press Ltd,
Lymington, Hants

Printed in Great Britain by
Clays Ltd, St Ives plc

for Maxine

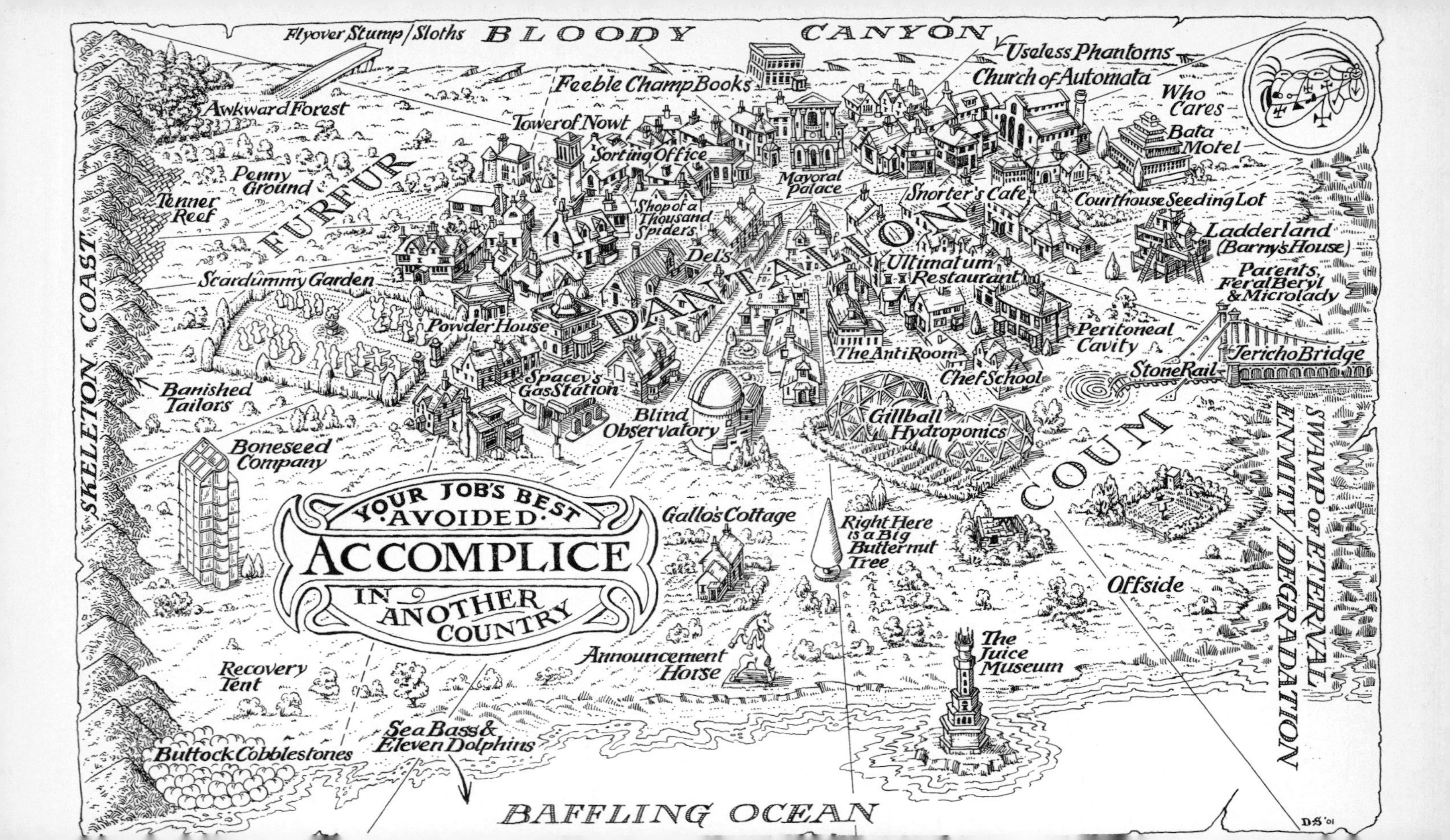

BLOODY CANYON
Flyover Stump/Sloths
Useless Phantoms
Feeble Champ Books
Church of Automata
Who Cares
Awkward Forest
Tower of Nowt
Bata Motel
Sorting Office
Penny Ground
FURFUR
Mayoral Palace
Tenner Reef
Shop of a Thousand Spiders
Snorter's Cafe
Courthouse Seeding Lot
DANTALION
Ladderland (Barny's House)
Del's
Ultimatum Restaurant
Scardummy Garden
Parents, Feral Beryl & Microlady
Powder House
Peritoneal Cavity
The AntiRoom
Jericho Bridge
Stone Rail
Chef School
Banished Tailors
Spacey's Gas Station
Blind Observatory
Gillball Hydroponics
Boneseed Company
COUM
SKELETON COAST
SWAMP OF ETERNAL ENMITY/DEGRADATION
YOUR JOB'S BEST AVOIDED
ACCOMPLICE
IN ANOTHER COUNTRY
Gallo's Cottage
Right Here is a Big Butternut Tree
Offside
The Juice Museum
Announcement Horse
Recovery Tent
Sea Bass & Eleven Dolphins
Buttock Cobblestones
BAFFLING OCEAN
DS '01

'Woken by searchlights in a soaked field,
I began to wish I had never met the mime.'

– Ben Rictus
My Crunchy Past

1

The Idiot

Enthusiasm and coherence don't always go together

Maybe it was the mascara in the spaniel's eyes, or just dumb luck. Either way Barny was playing blithely with fire. As they passed the scary glare of the creepchannel entrance, the dog began laughing so hard the mascara was blotching with tears and Barny knelt to check it out. Behind him, sour light needled from the creepchannel mouth like a drench of ice and vinegar.

And the dog Help had always been a strange one. He could shuffle all his fur down to one end of his body, sit upright in a chair like a human, whistle after women, and attack anyone who started singing in a sprightly manner. He'd clamp his jaws and hold on, looking up at you silent and rueful of this unwanted intimacy. His ears turned blue and flowed like water. The butter-wouldn't-melt mischief of his species had reached its pinnacle with Help. So it was no great surprise to Barny when he slipped his leash and did a runner into the stewing vortex.

Kicking through emeralds, Barny ascended the little slope, passed a beached and tilted grandfather clock and entered the demonic transit system. Of course he was instantly assailed by searing pain, stickled spinelight and corrosive etheric bile, but he was thinking about his dad's birthday. Pa Juno had been complaining about some undulant psychic parasite in his shack. Classic poltergeist activity and everyone was sure it was the ghost of his hair come back to mock him. Pa didn't go for that but Barny thought if he could help snare it using a Spitain Box or something, domestic order could be restored. Barny wasn't one to push out his belly and claim it was a stormfront – that kind of public mischief he left to Prancer Diego. Barny knew trouble was already in the mix, and had said so to Edgy one time. They'd been browsing in the Shop of a Thousand Spiders and Barny picked up a Vanta grid, which closed on his hand and forced a volley of curses from his gob. It was amid this volley that he conveyed the notion of trouble being in the mix. Edgy tore the shirt off a passing customer and offered it to Barny as a bandage, at which the customer barrelled into them with both fists in front of him like diesel buffers. A while later Barny and Edgy were shambling down the street like shattered puppets, but still Edgy was a happy man, gustily breathing the warm Accomplice air. 'Head securities, Bubba,' he said. 'That's the bottom line. Adopt a head. It's a stellar choice. Mine's right there on the register.'

Barny glanced at Edgy's head, thinking it looked like a hairy knife. 'Mean your ideas?'

'No – the head, Bubba, the head. The meat. You give a trade description of your head with its age and condition and it all goes into the index, which everyone ignores. Only a madman would check the prices. I can't believe anyone knows about it but me. Ah, what a beautiful day Bubba.' He squinted up at the trees. 'I doubled my money the first six weeks. And I spent the whole of that six weeks crying, and rubbing my face.'

'What's good about that?'

'I told you, I *doubled* my money. You can still make a bundle in this town if you keep your face and so on in good condition.'

But as ever in trying to help a friend Edgy had made a sacrifice – what with the damage to his nasal septum from the enraged customer, his entire head was devalued. So Edgy was still ensconsed at the Bata Motel, hanging on to his room by pretending to be a ghost. And it seemed to Barny that with this sort of stuff occurring without provocation, trouble needn't be sought out. All he wanted was to care for the winged and stepping animals of the earth and be happy.

Barny's distraction ended when, slipping in tubeway sputum, he couldn't get his hands out of his pockets fast enough to break his fall – he slammed his skull on the creepchannel's icy floor. Pain can't be wounded, as Violaine said, and here it blended with the howling atmosphere.

But as Barny's eyes focused, he saw padding across the frost a pair of beautiful white feet – there was a girl, ducking under spite icicles and looking back once as Barny sat up. Where had he seen her before? She climbed into a phosphene blot which showed intermittent flayed shavings of a hallway, cupboards, filigree. Barny looked around him at the pulsing vessels of the subway wall, which were encrusted with blown clocks, lawyers and other detritus. The blot had faded like a bruise by the time he stood.

Up ahead was a sunken car, poison drumming its roof. Turns in the tunnels showed frying glimpses of exit domains. Rigging and rind swayed from the ceiling. Barny picked up a steel head bucket and thought of taking it home as a feedbox for the leopard. That little cutey had swiped him hard in the chest the other day, bless him.

But he dropped it when a tumble of bugs caught his attention. They were rolling out of a valve, glittering down the wall and across the tunnel floor, where they pooled around a chest of drawers in the shadows. Drawing closer in the yellow light, Barny found an eye amid the flow, blinking. Below this was a rail of teeth. Stepping back, he detected the form of some kind of crocodilian caught in the melted pizza cheese of the channel wall. How long had the poor snapper been here? Barny tore aside the thick webbing, scalding his hands. 'You're sick,' he said, getting a good look at the reptile, and took it around the middle, dragging it off the shelf. Nerve-wire stretched behind it, snapping. 'You're a crazy 'gator,' whispered Barny, setting it down. 'An eight-footer. Wait till the guys at the office get a loada you.' The 'gator thrashed sluggishly as he secured the leash, but seemed to be coming around.

When Barny emerged from the creepchannel all begrained with gore and apocalypse dust, seaweed hanging from his ears, the predator was slowly regaining its curiosity. The dog Help was capering round a nearby tree. Barny was one pest up on the deal. What a find!

'Is a thing most fully itself in the darkness or the light?' In a vaulted cave the size of an aircraft hangar, Sweeney strummed his white gills thoughtfully. His fiddling imperial exoskeleton was bound by tender gut to a giant hull seat from which he was released when digestion allowed. A network of coaxial plasm cables fanned from the throne to phantom bandwidths. Sweeney thought about umbilical soda and painted bones and revisionists cooked in their shells as he gazed about him at the gallery of lank, raglike faces and the immense walls riddled with channel vents like withered waspcells. Nerve storms crackled in the altitudes of the roofing. 'I say: why add to something that's fine to begin with.'

The cook approached down a fatty ramp. Sweeney noted without optimism that he was spattered with green paint and carrying something angular on a giant dish. The cook placed it on a side table. When Sweeney blinked, little jaws flashed together instead of eyelids. 'What the hell do you call this?'

'I call it "Replacement Alligator of Boxes, in Green", for Your Majesty's pleasure.'

'Well there's little enough pleasure to be had here, it's made of boxes, man, boxes. What's this? "Wheaties". And none in there. What's the meaning of it all?'

'I feel it symbolises the power of casual disregard. A cool man is different from a cool day. For a start, he's smaller. Then there's the matter of acceptance—'

The cook's eyes boiled and sputed. His gurgling face fell like a hangnail as shrike branches rushed upward, splitting him like sliced bread. Then he exploded with cackling anatomies which shot legs and fiddled his pieces away into the corners. Sweeney was already calling down the Ruby Aspict, a bloody jewel which lowered through thunder. Veins and heart-rind made spirals in its slow rotation. 'Show me what happened to the 'gator,' he said thoughtfully. The crimson compound eye flooded the cavern with arterial light as Dietrich Hammerwire entered. 'What do you make of this?' Sweeney asked him.

Dietrich raised his wet anvil head. In the Aspict deeps a figure picked through an upper creepchannel. 'Not much meat on him.'

'Nothing was triggered, Dietrich – no shrikes, no nerve snares – look at him.'

They regarded the moon-faced moron calling 'Help!' in an inquiring, sing-song voice. 'Old shaman's trick, that cry. Distress camouflage.'

'Yes, no real fear in it.' Sweeney sat back and clattered a mandible down his ribs like a stick down a picket fence. 'Well this fellow entered the channel and improved the shining hour by stealing my lunch. You know how bland souls are these days, I'm having to marinate them in the nerve nets for days to give them any flavour. They haven't the imagination to be horrified half the time.'

'We should involve their legs a lot more. People don't like their legs interfered with.'

'You and your legs. No seriously, I was looking forward to it – that particular channel had the ambitions of a million paralegals flash-frozen into a stain in the walls, you can just taste it, can't you? Well, let's get our thief a name, shall we?'

Barny's name chimed from the guts of the Aspict.

Sweeney knew he needn't fear this Barny Juno. He had a specific vision of the man, or beast, he should fear. It had been foretold by good old Bingo Violaine years ago. Sweeney had been eating the philosopher's brain from his head and as the lower brain functions collapsed Violaine had begun yammering loudly through a heavy nosebleed. Dietrich was there and he and Sweeney often joked about Violaine's predictions, until they started coming true. This was the problem with tilling through someone's synaptic soup – the soul's a thread through the head and under threat it'll squirm into itself like a burning hair strand, ending as an untraceable atom without ego, breath or danger. Nobody else's business anyway. The solvent stench of old resentments will distract while you pack up and shoot into the drywall. Violaine survived in this form – he's telling you so.

'There we are,' said Sweeney, ratcheting his shoulders in a shrug. 'This Barny fellow, you'll have to pop above and eat the cobwebbed cherries of his heart, I think. Bring the reptile here and do a sort of spangly tumbling act when you arrive, for m'pleasure.'

'Me? Not Trubshaw?' Dietrich ventured, thinking of the chaos above. 'Or Kermit?'

'Skittermite's stuck in a drain and Trubshaw's a monster.'

'That's what I mean,' protested Dietrich. 'I *know* he is.'

'You're the fiend for the job Dietrich, and you're starting to annoy. So get out – and take the hanging loops of your venom delivery system with you.'

2

Dead Letters

To smoke a cigar while being tortured is the ultimate gesture

Sweating like a bastard, Gregor jogged heavily up the wooden ramp, pressed himself against the front door and whispered Barny's name. The door opened and Barny stood there, next to the lion. The animal was doing the snaggle-toothed motion of his mouth and head which had inflicted so much turmoil on Gregor's pants since its rescue from Karloff's Circus a month ago. 'We're in for a storm,' said Barny almost inaudibly amid the chatter of monkeys. He began laughing in the delight of his activities. 'I'm rearing cochineal beetles on prickly pear cactus to produce the red dye used in campari. Edgy's idea.' The aspirin eyes of lizards winked in the swirling dark behind him. 'Cash cow. And the geckos love 'em.'

A rotund pebble of a man, Gregor whimpered a little, then pointed to what he thought were the outer facts but which were actually ensconsed behind his eyes. 'Barny. You can't keep this lion here.'

'Doesn't it have integrity?'

'Integrity? The point is it's a mammal and I know you understand that. There's just no telling. Look out you bastard.'

'Calm down Gregor – rest on its head now.'

'No fear.'

'Eh?'

'I said I'm damned if I'll "rest on its head" as you put it. Are you stupid? Mad?'

'Don't follow you, Round One.'

'Don't call me that. Oh, I'm in hell.'

'There, there.'

'Get away from me.'

'I was just putting my arm round you.'

'Like hell you were. I don't know what to say about it all.'

'What do you mean?'

'You. Standing there in front of the lion.'

'So what? In his mouth a body tastes much the same as it would in yours.'

'What the hell?' Gregor didn't know whether to ram or run. As a distraction from his woes, Barny held his own hazards.

'Pop round the back, Gregor, there's something that'll interest you.'

'He'll drag me apart,' Gregor added as Barny closed the door on the lion, and they walked around the side of the house.

'Just waiting for Golden Sid then I'm off. What you doing here anyway?'

'Nothing really, got a little problem,' Gregor muttered. 'Thought if I went for an early run, people would see me and think I was a healthy man who knew what he was doing.'

'We can go in to work together then,' said Barny as they entered the half of the perspex hothouse which had once been the home of a green iguana called Mister Spiderman. This web-throated lovely had gone to heaven and Barny had buried him in a ceremony which caused outrage among the local doll men and powderheads. 'I'm damned,' Barny had said, 'if I'm going to fire Mister Spiderman out of a cannon.' Protesters had turned up at the funeral and Barny's picture ended up in the paper because his trousers fell down as he read the eulogy.

'There he is,' he said now, gesturing to the reptile on the terrarium floor. The 'gator turned half around, hissed at Gregor, and closed its mouth with a wet slap. 'The food rips as he shuts his gob. Look at him, sleek as a Mazaratti. I'm gunna need bigger reptile lights for this charmer.'

'Barny? How can you think this is normal?'

'I don't know, what, was I wrong? If I'm wrong I stand corrected I suppose.' Barny crouched to attach a leash to the reptile. 'Anyway, think of it as a dinosaur. They're great value, Gregor. What did Violaine say – "Everything is an advantage to the indiscriminate".'

'It's nothing like a dinosaur,' Gregor groaned. 'I wish it was.'

'Everyone loves dinosaurs,' said Barny, not hearing him.

'Not like me. I love them.'

'We all do, Gregor.'

'I mean, really love them.'

'So you keep telling me, it's all settled.'

'You're not listening, Barny, this is the problem I mentioned earlier. I really – you know – *really* love them. I mean, big trousers and all.'

'What?' Barny straightened up.

'You know.'

'Big trousers you said.' Barny stared at him a while. 'And you're casting asparagus at *me*? Dinosaurs? You'll accomplish a reputation you bastard, like Dot Spacey at the gas station. I don't understand. D'you even care if they're male or female?'

Gregor hung his head, gloomily abashed. 'Not really.'

'They're *dinosaurs*, Gregor. Look, I don't want to continue with this discussion, it's planting a pain behind my face. See a doctor or something, you see? Here's Golden Sid at last. Don't say any more.'

A man like a startled ant in buff overalls, Golden Sid went the gangplank route around the house, flinching at every screech and wall-bang from within. A lot of the houses around here were built on stilts due to the floods of snot which roared down the street from the chef school. 'Hey, Sid,' Gregor muttered as they passed, and Sid gave a weak smile, pathetically grateful for any encounter which did not end in violence. Pop-eyed and bespectacled, he tarried on the yard platform until Barny, Gregor and the alligator had shuffled into the street, then leant against the door, breathing deep as before a dive, eyes closed.

He threw open the door and entered, already screaming.

As the 'gator wallowed across the hot tarmac, Gregor chatted absently about tomorrow's ball game but he was clearly distracted. The day was humid and fertile, masonry flaking amid hard plants and salty air. A Gubba Man stood on a corner, a black nebula of ants glittering its face. Rib spirals stood here and there, the result of stray boneseed spores.

Passing through the centre of town, Barny and Gregor led the 'gator across the main square. Here was a statue of Bingo Violaine on the site of the bandstand where the philosopher died, inconveniently clawed underground by a white devil. An inscription on the plinth read: TRY TO ACCEPT THAT INTELLIGENCE IS ABOARD. Other folk on their way to work never gave it a glance but Barny liked sometimes to climb the figure and swing on its punching arm. From here he could see the distant bone wall, the swamplands, turquoise glimpses of ocean. The ashes of a tailor gusted from a darkened patch near the steps of the mayoral palace, the shadow of last night's revelries.

All this roofed a blind underworld of poison light which nobody recalled until they blundered in. The creepchannel network was side-on to sight, a bandwidth away, sick and aglow. Demons blurred through it like subway trains going elsewhere. The sundrenched land above was small fry.

Down an alley and through a side door – Barny, Gregor and the 'gator descended iron steps to the sorting office. It was a low-ceilinged basement, slick with condensation. From above, a delivery chute fed the long black tongue of the sorting table, which bisected the chamber and could not be ignored. One dirty lightbulb hung into this wedge-shaped cell, picking out a few bony chairs. Shelves of plate fungus held impoverished ornaments to the wall, withered attempts to make the place more homey. The ornaments, too, were made of fungus and the only way to personalise them was to dope the spores with cells from the workers' bodies. It was similar to the boneseed principle used in Accomplice architecture. But the figurines produced were of such intensely subconscious significance to one and all that they became yet another subject to evade. On the opposite wall a flat fungus like a massive starfish spread from corner to corner, pullulating at the centre. When I say that this was the drinks dispenser, you will understand the state of despairing extremity persisting in that place.

When Barny's co-workers clapped eyes on the reptile it was like he'd hefted in a godsize flounder and whapped it across their faces. They stood in gratifyingly varied stances of appalled incomprehension, and to Barny's loving eyes their opinions unfurled like flowers.

'It's moving.'

'Doomed – I'm scared I'm—'

'The weirdest since the landcrab.'

'Look – he's saying it's his friend.'

'No stopping him.'

'Like he doesn't have a choice.'

'I can't believe he doesn't know.'

'Got a crazy man on our little hands.'

'It's real. I've just understood.'

'Keep him talking and I'll throw the lid.'

'Village idiot with snarling trump card.'

'I'll have the roast beef platter.'

'Repeatedly fails in the harmless department.'

B.B. Henrietta squinted back and forth from Barny to the reptile. 'You don't give up, do you? This fucking animal?'

'You need to take a nap, Bubba,' said Edgy, standing like a ragged exclamation mark. 'We'll take care of this little problem.'

'I found him in a loada slime,' said Barny, looking proud. 'I'm a lucky bum, I know it.'

'I'll throw the lid now,' whispered Fang, and tried flinging a hubcap at Barny, but the boxing gloves he wore hindered the procedure and it clanged straight at the floor near the stone steps. Fang looked gloomy, and sat down at the sorting table.

'A reptile can be powerfully hostile to your passerby, Bubba.'

'I told him already,' said Gregor, lumbering in with a pile of timber. 'But I'm starting to get used to it. And you can bet the Blaze'll get off on the monster.'

Barny hadn't thought of his girlfriend's response. She'd think he was reckless and love it. He felt another door slam on clear understanding.

'Keep your mind on the game, Round One. It's low to the ground, Bubba.'

'I know, like a drophead. They're slower and less aggressive than crocs.'

'Bless. And the tail's sorta squared off, Bubba, top and sides. Almost looks mechanical.'

'The tail's perfect, of course. It downright makes me want to cry.'

'All right,' said B.B. Henrietta, holding up her hands. 'You guys can stand there crying about the shape of that animal's tail as long as you like. I have a job to do.'

'Mister Spiderman was a herbivore – I'll need to sort a diet for Mister Newton here. And I'm making a diagram of his head.'

'Good for you, a diagram,' said Gregor, opening the furnace.

'Well this is no ordinary diagram, Round One. It'll show the charm of the skull and inner nostril circumstances for everyone to understand. You see, the head's flat like a pike. The 'gator has one of the longest brains in nature.'

'Longest,' said Edgy. 'Did you said "Mister Newton" before?'

'I said so because that's the creature's full name.' Barny tethered the reptile and sat at the sorting table. 'Boy, I've done it now. And I couldn't have without Help.'

'Oh, you mean mascara boy.'

'Mascara?' asked Henrietta, toying with a package.

'Barny's dog wears mascara.'

'How could you *do* that, Bubba?'

'He doesn't – he says the dog applies it.'

'How?'

'Nobody knows. He's never seen it happen. Who understands the ways of dogs? It's possible Help's some kind of celebrity in the dog world, and has to keep up appearances at all times. Maybe he's a male prostitute. Or perhaps he just likes to look good.'

'He doesn't look good to me.'

'Of course not, B.B. But he feels good about himself, and that's important. Hey Barny that reminds me – I spoke to my friend who works at the publishers, they're after someone to do a book about dog experiences. I told them to all intents and purposes you are one.'

Past bestsellers from Feeble Champ Books had been an account of fanatical ear-varnishing, *Nothing Sacred*, and a study of man/rhino love, *Never Again*.

'I don't know how to write a book.'

'I'll ghost it for you.'

'Really?'

'What's not to ghost? I could even add some personal touches – I've had a few dog experiences of my own, you know.' Edgy smirked scampishly. 'They're thinking of calling it *My Dog Friends*. There could be a rich oil painting on the cover of me smiling with my arm round the shoulders of an Alsatian, something like that.'

'Why'd they want a picture of you?' asked Gregor, sitting down. Edgy muttered to Barny, and took him aside for a word.

'Listen Barny,' he whispered. 'Here's the main business. The Round One's got a problem. With dinosaurs.'

'He was telling me about it, I didn't know what to say.'

'We can help him.'

'I don't think so. Not this time.'

'He's besotted. He needs to purge it away, express himself by consummating these feelings. I went to Doctor Perfect and pretended to have Gregor's symptoms, okay? He said I was crazy, a bastard, sick, a threat to society. He actually said I reminded him of himself when he was younger. Then he kicked me over, and over and over again, calling me a poison. He said he, er, "relinquished all responsibility", that was it. Told me to go out and just do whatever I had to do.'

'With a dinosaur? Where?'

'Well, there's the museum.'

'The Juice Museum?'

'No, Bubba, the dry one with the bones. I've seen them in there, big girls too. Hadrosaurs.'

'But they're skeletons, I don't understand. They're dinosaurs, Edgy.'

'You bet. I might even have a go at one myself.'

'But that's—'

'Necrophilia I know, but can you see a live Tyrannosaur around here Bubba?' He glanced back at Gregor sitting under the bulb, and continued in hushed tones. 'It's lucky Gregor can distinguish between a T-Rex and a 'gator or we'd maybe have the sickest ever paternity suit on our nervy hands my friend. We need him on form tomorrow. You, me and Gregor are busting into the museum tonight.'

Barny was about to protest when a tumble of objects crashed down the chute – the stuff already radiated dread and anxiety into the office. Looking down, Gregor seemed about to cry.

It just kept coming, every day. Miscellaneous objects wrapped in paper and card. Magazines. Notes and forms full of writing. But none of it related to anyone here in the basement. Nothing was mentioned but strangers and their obscure affairs. Why were these objects turning up? What did it all mean? And what, above all, was expected of them here?

They had devised a number of means of disposal. Some they burnt as they covered their faces with rags. Other stuff they tried to eat. The big objects they sculpted into an angular sentinel in a conical hat, which they pelted with cans until everyone became sort of embarrassed and fell silent. Fang would stuff it all in a car boot and drive it over a cliff. Gregor had taken to baking the things in a high-tech ceramics kiln. He would remove the ingredients before the process was complete and form this mush into a poultice for his arse. Near the cabinet was an open corner, a stale etheric fold gaping into seemingly bottomless space – this blot of shadow they called the Drop and it was invaluable, swallowing just about all the stuff they could dump there. But throughout they suspected there was something more specific and important they should be doing with it all, and sometimes, in private, they wept with the build-up of sheer, unspoken stress. At other times one of the group would go into a hysterical screaming jag at the unstoppable flow of stuff sliding down the chute from above. They never openly communicated their doubts. Inadequacy, depression and fear of discovery grained the gloomy air.

'Well,' said Edgy, unbuttoning his Hawaiian shirt and fetching the scarification gear. 'Let's get to work.'

When the Captain entered an hour later, the office had sunk to a level of savage superstition. Edgy was blowing a bone whistle and hanging back from a rawhide cord skewered to the tenting flesh of his chest. Gregor was bent in worship before a papier-mâché effigy of a normal fella and Barny had begun screaming in a demented way, frightening himself with his intensity. Fang was cooking pasta, an ominous look on his face. Gregor stood to attention with a hysterical giggling which tumbled over into wrenching sobs – he tore aside and hid his face against the wet wall. 'The boys are sorry, Captain,' said B.B. Henrietta, who was sat at the table wearing a useless wooden helmet. 'They're upset about . . . the election. Fang's been told he can't vote because he's all dead and going to slurry.' In the daylight hours Fang refused to behave like a scary revenant and found it hurtful when certain people still didn't accept him.

'We're all excited about the election, lads,' stated the Captain, frowning. Bloodshot eyes were turning from their inner torment to focus slowly upon him. Gregor had sunk down the wall and clung there like a workhouse orphan. 'But I answer to Mr Gibbon. There are quotas to be filled in this important time and that's what you know. Are those bats?' The Captain framed this as a question, though he could see the bats quite clearly near the ceiling. By parsing the data this way he planned to draw the workers out of what appeared to be a back alley suicide pact and into an informal but constructive dialogue. Though the Captain was completely in the dark as to the purpose of the office, he was no fool. It took expert management to employ a zombie wearing boxing gloves and get away with it.

'I'm part-time here,' said Barny, shuffling forward a little.

'That's right, er, Barny. These bats, boys, now I'm as liberal as the next man of course.'

'I'm part-time here,' Barny choked, grimacing as he approached.

'Yes, yes you are. Now come on, lads – bats I mean now.'

'I'm part-time here!' Barny shrieked, throwing himself into the Captain's arms and hanging limp, emitting raw sobs like a castaway.

The Captain threw him off. 'Can't you see I don't give a damn about that? I'd prefer to know how these bats got in here. What have you guys been up to?'

'We need them for company, Captain.'

'Well for the sake of all that's pure you can't have a conversation with those mothers can you.'

'We kiss them Captain,' Fang volunteered. 'It gets awful lonely down here.'

'Is that why those wooden chairs are drawn up to the corners?'

'For standing on. Then we purse our lips and kiss those little beauties on their snouts.'

'They enjoy it,' said Gregor. 'They start quivering all over.'

'And staring,' added Fang. 'As if they can't believe their luck.'

'Captain,' sighed Edgy dreamily, squinting slowly aside from his tilted suspension. Dark blood coated his chest. 'Me and the Round One need a half day tomorrow.'

'For the local semi I suppose,' nodded the Captain, a little uncomfortable. 'All right. Give 'em hell.'

'You're a good man,' Edgy rasped, and the skin of his chest broke, allowing him to fall to the concrete floor in a state of total exhaustion.

'I don't need to tell you how to do your jobs,' the Captain stated firmly, ignoring the sudden sharp looks the statement provoked, 'but it's come to my attention that—'

And turning on his heels, he trotted up the stairs and slammed out.

'I wish he wouldn't do that,' muttered Fang. But there was

a flood of feeling in the room when they realised that the alligator, sitting utterly still near the shredder, had gone unnoticed and forgotten until the doorslam sent it into a surprised frenzy of thrashing, hissing and quite frank and open biting of three staff members, each of whom screamed at the top of their lungs that there was no saviour local enough to take away this pain.

The leopard sprang upward, swiping, and snagged Sid's trouser leg. The cat hung a moment, its screech dopplering like a race hog, and fell back into the kitchen. Golden Sid clambered on to the rain-lashed roof and dropped the hatch closed, his shredded clothes flying with water. Sobbing and babbling, he stumbled on the teeming slope as a burst of lightning freaked the sky. Something banged on to the roof behind him and he squinted around at a form feathered with shadows, folding into itself and stepping forward. Wings tucked behind a metallic bone soldier hung with surgical tubing. 'Mind if we have a natter,' said the stone beak which prowed from the head's hanging varicose tangle. Sid could tell with a doomed acceptance that this was the sort of over-familiar ghoul who'd think nothing of stabbing you with its chin. On his knees, he watched it approach – a lattice of biological junk barely contained by clawed ribs which blurred and stretched through the rain on his glasses. Then the creature's sternum opened like a wet rose and threw something at him.

Dietrich shook the storm from his plasmic hair and watched the roiling trees as Sid twitched, a nerve cable strung from the centre of his forehead.

3

Boner

The stumbling idiot may evade the traps

Barny and Plantin Edge sauntered through the dark museum, their steps and the slap-shuffle of the 'gator reverberating down the hallways. Gregor had run ahead to the Cretaceous section.

Rows of cases contained bones as fragile as antique combs.

'Boy, these critters are really thin.'

'They're skeletons Barny, remember? I can't believe you brought the 'gator here.'

'Don't you think it'll be an education for the lad, seeing his ancestors all done up in scaffolding and so on.'

'Would you be educated? What if your dad was here, all dried out?'

'He'd ask me what the hell I was doing.'

'And what would you learn?'

'Nothing, I admit. You know, my father's got a problem with his hair. It's haunting him.'

'Why, what's the problem?'

'I told you, it's haunting him. You know a bit about this stuff Edgy, can you help me pick up a trap at the Shop tomorrow?'

'I'll tell you what, Bubba,' said Edgy with a touch of reverence, stopping everything. They'd turned a corner to confront the frozen snarl of a stuffed sabre-tooth tiger on a pedestal. 'Maybe there's a lesson here after all.'

'Like what.'

'Stress, Bubba. Remember they always say it's caused by the old "fight or flight" response, which in primitive times was meant to save cavemen from the tigers? But today it's got no outlet, causing ill-health. And that's where you come in, my friend.'

'How?'

'By re-introducing the tiger factor. People round here can't walk the street without the very real terror you'll take one of the big cats for a walk again. Remember when the lion attacked Dot Spacey at the gas station? He actually laughed at first. And he couldn't molest the vehicles for a whole month afterward. People need a little danger.' They wandered past the skeleton of one of the Steinway Spiders, a ribbed piano with bony legs. 'So they seek it out. You know the Patently Damaging Sports Club? That's the kinda thing I'm talking about. Dangerous activities like, uh . . . driving a car at top speed while being knifed by a crazy midget. Or slamming your face against a concrete abutment while gulping some brand of poison. Wow, Bubba. I'd give anything to join. But it's exclusive membership, all very shady, you know. You have to wait to be approached by a member who reckons you're the right stuff.'

'I heard Neville Peth's a member. He drove a sort of burning trolley van across a traffic island.'

'Neville Peth? Guess which course of exhaustion he favours.'

'I don't know.'

'He's a financial adviser. Office across from Spacey's station.' In fact Neville Peth was a specialist in dove insurance – Accomplice citizens were regularly injured or killed by small groups of doves. 'You see, Barny? All walks of life. Well, I guess I might let him happen to see what a clumsy risk-taker I can be, eh Bubba?'

They stood before a stand bearing a grey pineapple of hard dust. 'What's this?' asked Barny.

'Drylord seed. Don't touch it.'

'I've never seen one,' Barny muttered, and tapped it lightly. It released a puff of dandruff.

'See, Bubba?' Edgy smirked. 'You would have missed that little glory if you'd gone to your parents' tonight. You should get out, see more of the world.' A piercing klaxon alarm exploded through the establishment and Edgy grabbed his arm. 'We're done for. We'll be explaining it all to a judge – this one, probably.' He pointed at the egg. 'Run, you idiot.'

'What about Gregor?' asked Barny as they ran, the reptile in their arms like a rolled carpet.

'The Round One can sprint away from anything – it's his special gift.'

The demon perched on the family home like a designer label. Dietrich had learnt precious little from the quailing unfortunate on Barny's roof. Normally the shock of fear pushed the salient from the victim in a gutburst, but this poor guy seemed to have been deliberately conditioned into such a pitch of terror already, the facts emerged in a dribble. Even this sample was mostly incoherent, though Dietrich had established that Barny was due to visit his folks in the swamp tonight. The only other dreg to come through concerned a rumour. Some jokers in the town had been going on about Barny looking after 'eight hundred eels' in his garden. Apparently they were so persistent about it they even had Barny convinced, in his weaker moments. Eight hundred eels in his garden. And none of this was true. Dietrich looked out across the swamp – an object tangy and steaming like something spilt on a kitchen floor – and knew once again why he disdained the world of man.

The shack was a shabby porched affair but the gutters were sturdy. Dietrich hung upside-down and peered in the window at an illumined tableau of marital exasperation. With his demon eyes he could see something silver in the air, flowing like a watersnake – the couple seemed unaware of it. In the corner was a canary cage in which a squeaky perch was swinging. On the perch was a moth. The woman cast frequent fond glances at this.

They were sat in concrete rocking chairs. The old man smoked a pipe into which he pushed a few crackling bugs. The old woman read a newspaper called the *Blank Stare*. Their conversation, as related to the demon Sweeney at a later date, went like this:

Mrs: Says here the Mayor's out kissing babies.
Mr: He been caught?
Mrs: I mean door-to-door in the ancient style.
Mr: Saw the Mayor with a baby once. Held it like a rifle. Took me right back.
Mrs: In the land of the blind the one-eyed man fears the snakes.
Mr: Before long he'll be outta there lugging a case tied shut with an extension cord.
Mrs: He'll pull some stunt at the Parade like he always does. And he's planning to drone on about statues this time. Why don't we go to the Garden as a family any more?
Mr: Last week we went. You kept going on about the girl statues.
Mrs: They were everywhere, including that Blaze woman. Someone should take a hammer to her dummy.
Mr: That's statucide, Ethel. All remote the formal buildings of punishment, eh? The girl's not worth it.
Mrs: She'll strip him to a skeleton and shoot him through a hoop.
Mr: Well, she hasn't moved in at least. Last time I was there I spent a good hour getting clobbered by the hose-like face of an aardvark. Yeah, the snozzle of one.
Mrs: He's not happy unless he's sitting around with the winged and stepping animals of the earth.
Mr: Anything goes with that guy.
Mrs: What are you getting so steamed up about? He's your son, you should be thrilled to bits he doesn't lick his own eyes like a gekko.
Mr: Fine, I'm going to fish.
Mrs: Go fish then.
Mr: There's nothing fierce enough to be worth the catching.

Mrs: In the world?
Mr: The swamp, Ethel, the swamp, have you looked lately? Even the doves are slimy round here. On the porch the other night – heard the motorised buzz of a horseshoe crab. *That's* how low we've sunk in the world.
Mrs: Ideal thoughts teach us what we needn't expect.
Mr: And so what if he can't lick his own eyes? You rather your son lick the eyes of a stranger? Aren't you haunted by that idea?
Mrs: We both know perfectly well what haunts *you*, Henry.
Mr: Fine, I'm going to fish.
Mrs: Go fish then.
Mr: There's nothing fierce enough to be worth the catching.
Mrs: In the world?

It went on like this for hours and Dietrich Hammerwire began to feel that the centuries he'd spent in the hellish catacombs were a lovely, lucky dream. He'd been led into the most fiendish, mindless of blind alleys. Barny never showed.

Edgy spat aside on to the bleak forehead of a crow. Rearranging his crotch, he hunkered on the mound.

'They still there, Palatino?' sneered G.I. Bill.

Edgy had always claimed his balls detached and flew away at night, returning at dawn all begrimed with moss and lemongrass. Gregor once said Edgy went on about this to keep his women alert. 'Alert?' Edgy had snorted, looking distastefully at Gregor. 'You've got a lot to learn about women.'

'Keep your face on the game, Billy,' he told G.I., whose face in fact signalled a detour from the species.

'You'll pay for tearin' my shirt that time, Palatino.'

'Quit flappin' your gills, doughboy. Let it go.'

Not much chance of that. G.I. Bill put on his clothes each morning without taking any off the previous night, so that he bloated out over the weeks until the moment the authorities forcibly undressed the bastard. Today he was the size of a bouncy castle and the shirt was at the heart of it. 'You shouldn't oughtn't to have done it, Pal.'

'So regret me. Hey Bubba, where's the Round One? You on line?'

Down the far end of the field, Barny swung the guppy stick absently. 'I'm worried about the leopard,' he called. 'He's moody.'

'Moody leopard or not, keep your face on the game,' Edgy shouted. 'We're missing our runner, where is the bastard?'

'Maybe behind bars, skimming cards into a hat.'

'What's wrong with the leopard?' yelled Edgy.

'Something spooked him,' Barny hollered. 'Sid too.' Barny related how Golden Sid had woven his screams into an aural tapestry in which some bleak envoy landed on the roof and was limbering up for a freakish procedure when Sid snapped with the strain. And apparently it was pissing down the entire time.

G.I. Bill and his team looked on in disgust. 'Can we get on with this?' Bill demanded, hefting a battered leather bag which knocked and jounced in his hands. Inside was a grade-A veggy ball with a sick little mind of its own, capable of flying by its own steam and spurting unnecessary slime at one and all. On release, the name of the game was to avoid this gilled abomination at all costs. Dodgers, screamers, runners and hitters made up the team, and upon every player in a team being accosted, that team lost. Everyone was here but Gregor. And their dodger, the mechanic Mike Abblatia, had a bad back that was swelling.

'You think Gregor's still in the dinosaur era?' Edgy bellowed.

'That's it,' said G.I. Bill with finality, and opened the bag.

'It's like Bingo said,' Edgy remarked jauntily as they entered the Cretaceous section, 'the great man carries a number of auxiliary morals of his own devising.'

'Why is Gregor a great man?' Barny asked, leading the 'gator. Since it pulled a U-ey and snapped Fang on the noggin, Barny had been dressing it in a flowery skirt and hat for reasons which are still a mystery. Juno Theorists have claimed that he hoped these pastoral glories would percolate into the long brain of the reptile and serve as a balm to its savage instincts. In my capacity as a free-range spirit I can select which mind or object to inhabit at any one time and I'm sorry to say at that moment I was laughing it up in the whipping antennae of a tsetse fly. I was amused to see that the insect's knee was like the spring joint of a beanpod, but as to this skirt and hat business I'm a washout.

'By not showing up he won us the game. He's a champion, Bubba.'

'I thought he got stuck here last night,' said Barny, frowning. 'Isn't it why we're here, Plantin?'

'Oh, Barny boy.' Edgy lit a slim cigar. 'Sporting genius is a funny thing.'

'All right, well I'll look at the Iguanadon over there, it's giving me the thumbs-up.'

'Wait a minute Bubba.' Edgy pointed at a horned bone tank with classic plates and a skull the size of an engine block. 'Gregor's always had an eye for the ladies. This here Triceratops could see off the formidable Gorgosaurus with that armoured crest and disastrous horns. Take a look underneath, there's a thing like a mechanics' pit down there.'

'He's not in here,' Barny called, peering under, and stood to admire the proud face and beak. 'Look at that, Mister Newton. This Tops is like an alligator snapping turtle – bite like a giant hole punch.'

At this point the anti-dove insurer Neville Peth entered, spectacles glinting, holding a lunchbox. Edgy pitched his cigar aside, yelling, 'And that's exactly what I'm starting to do – because I'm an adrenalin junky, Bubba.'

'Eh?'

Edgy was forcing his head into the dinosaur's gob, shouting, 'That's right – look at me placing everything I need at risk between the hazardous sharps of this – *Chhhhhrrriiiiisst*!' And he tore his head out again, staggering back.

Disappointed, Neville Peth turned and walked out.

'What's your Uncle Edgy doing now?' Barny asked the 'gator.

Edgy was jittering. 'I found the Round One, Bubba. That sick bastard's hiding in the skull of this monster. He musta crawled up through the neck cavity. He's stuck in there folded up like a boy.'

Barny sprang into action without thought for himself or anyone else.

In the eaves of the museum, Dietrich pinned himself open like a lab bat. He heard the approach of a gaggle of kids. Now was the moment to drop – and he saw this scene below: Barny Juno gesticulating at his scarecrow friend, scarecrow man hoisting up the reptile and waltzing awkwardly with it while screaming, and Juno taking a fire axe from the wall. As the crowd of kids entered and their terrified attention was claimed by the bad man dancing, Juno split a fossilised skull, which released a blathering, blob-faced tar baby. Its features were inlaid with teeth and softboiled eyes, and it seemed overcome with emotion. It hugged Juno.

In the acid night of Sweeney's throne room Dietrich substantiated his florid account by waving a copy of the *Blank Stare* which bore the headline: LARD-ARSE BORN FROM FOSSIL.

After the initial clang as he deployed his ears, Sweeney remained silent until the tale was told. Then he pursed his lips thoughtfully. This was preferable to Sweeney in a good mood as he had a spiral smile which operated like a Chinese finger trap, inescapable up to your shoulder.

'I seem to know the minutae of your failures, why is that?'

'Because you are with me in spirit, Your Majesty.'

'Yes but here's a man, some drawling layabout. I ask you to kill him in a broad, general way, and what happens?'

'Disaster, Your Majesty.'

'Well disaster's putting it a bit strong but here I am enthroned in a veined hull and so on, see what I mean? Out you go, and come back with a frankly dreary story about some shamanic chancer. I mean be ominous at least. What about the reptile?'

'He's patched it up.'

'The wisdom?'

'He hasn't asked it anything.'

'Is he a moron?'

'His attention seems to be elsewhere.'

The huge white beetle considered this. 'No, it's controlled folly. The man's a sorcerer. Think about it, half of what you gleaned from that screaming tosser on the roof was mere fancy, a planted lie. Even he probably didn't realise it. And when you go to the assigned destination you're treated to a stream of top-of-the-line bollocks from what were probably two unemployed actors doing him a favour. It all led you to a museum – there's a message in that. Raising the past, starting with the 'gator.'

'I thought dinosaurs became birds. Remember what Violaine said about creation? "If you're going to make something light, be sure it contains the important parts of something heavy." '

'Don't quote that bastard to me – wasn't he in here prophesying doom on all cylinders? While I ate his head like a herb? *God* Almighty!'

'Doom perhaps, but not by Juno's hand. Anyway no one gave a damn about Violaine till you crashed up through that bandstand and clawed him down in a spray of blood and gutwater. The crowd had actually been throwing pieces of flint till you did that, Your Majesty. Now he's everyone's favourite brainsaver. It worries me to hear you talk that way.'

'Well never mind Violaine. This fool, this lethal idiot you describe – he created a pig servant, at a public venue, before your eyes. What's he telling you? You aim to kill him and at that instant he raises life from death. He's laughing in our baked faces. No, we need a different strategy. Accomplice is bound in, knowing only itself. Pop 'em a rumour and it pinballs to a blur. The truth becomes an unattended sideshow. Morality? They wear the notion like a wig. We'll use the community against him, Dietrich. It's a long game but I like that sort of thing.'

'By your command.'

Dietrich took a face from the ancient gallery.

4

Transmission

Authority insists that misery is an education

The ornate blood clock was weighted into motion, two doors of red gold flipping open – from each a glossy figurine propelled into jerky battle, signalling the hour with a clash of swords. On the balcony above, the Mayor bellied out like a figurehead. He took a dim view of the town square – across which a lone figure drew a large sea chest – and returned inside. He called from his desk for the next dupe to be ushered in.

It turned out to be a towering, slack-faced man in a woollen hat and coat which seemed a needless extravagance in the day's wet heat. The man sat down in a studied way, as though the act were a foreign custom.

'Mr . . . Hammer is it? Mayor Rudloe. I suppose it's about the Parade?'

'I know nothing whatever about it. I've been sent with a proposition for you.' He looked aside at the balcony window. Clouds like a scattered jigsaw. 'Your little world here. It's icing on top and dead inside.'

'Well holy smokes man, we try. Denial's our middle name here in Accomplice. We positively flaunt our denial.' The Mayor broke off to throw a paperweight at a large floor lobster near the desk. These huge house insects, physical manifestations of corruption, infested the mayoral palace. 'And keep our moral fibre under armed guard. You know the tower across town? Like a lighthouse? It's housed there. Length of muscle, stretched between two pegs. I've seen it of course, as Mayor. Quite a sight. Twanged on the hour. I'd have it here if I could, but . . . tradition, you know.'

'You're in the manipulation business. I respect that. My master's taught me the current manner of things in this place. Said I'd need a special shirt and so on. When you speak to me, you speak to him.'

'Why do I want to, Mr Hammer? What are you offering?'

'I could put a cobweb on your wound, Mr Mayor. From me to you. You have an opposite in contest for power?'

'No one special – doomed Eddie Gallo is all.'

'Doomed Eddie Gallo.'

'Don't worry, the blossoming cancer of modesty blots any talents he may have, thank goodness. Armchair ideals. Kind. Feeble. Walks with his mouth. Stay away. My next platform'll be statues probably. Hell of a statue problem in this town. And then there's what I call my vacuum proposals. A Gubba Man on every corner. Stores that bite over your head. Work and get worse. Swerving's a no-no.'

'When driving?'

'Or walking. Think about it. Then there's guilt designation and so on. Yes, I expect another resounding mandate for my personal wealth.'

'And it's true people still bow to these institutions?'

'The dead branch still draws the water.'

The man didn't seem impressed by the Mayor's knowledge of Violaine philosophy and got down to business all the faster. 'My master can defeat more enemies for your meat dollar, Mr Mayor. He has knowledge of the perfect spanner in the works with which to crowbar your crowd. There's a man named Barny Juno whom you can quite easily portray as a threat to society.'

'Why would I do that?'

'Least importantly, because he is. He owns a stolen reptile which has and will injure the innocent. The reptile was stolen from my master and I'll require its return. More importantly for you Juno's the perfect target, a scapegoat for the ills of the area.'

'Well now that I know all this, why do I need you or your boss?'

'Endorsement, for one. Endless resources for another. He's what you'd call a demon. In fact, *the* demon.'

'You're saying that were I to meet this gentleman, I'd call him "the demon".'

'Yes.'

'And this is the man who wants to publicly endorse my campaign.'

'Suitably disguised, of course. As a goat-herd, say. Or a large, turmoiling maggot. A winner with the kids.'

'Maggot.' The Mayor steepled his hands in thought, then gave a little gasp of exasperation. 'Mr Hammer, I'm not sure you understand the . . . principles on which a political campaign is run. If this demon—'

'– *The* demon.'

'. . . er, *the* demon you refer to were to endorse me as his man for office, he, she or it would have to appear undisguised, otherwise what would be the point?'

'Well, he's very *similar* to a maggot. He's very pale, a kind of pale insect, if you like. But as strong as an ox, I assure you.'

'How is this all relevant?'

'Well, if the public at large were to clock him as he is, I'm not sure they could take the stress. Though he does go completely black occasionally, when he's in a mood. That might win some votes.'

'A poster campaign showing a jet black insect endorsing my candidacy.'

'He'll leave his carapace behind. He has to, anyway, when he comes above. Oh, and I should mention he can only emerge into your world when his bowels allow.'

'Thank you, Mr Hammer, for dropping by. I'm always happy to speak to members of my constituency on matters which concern them. Don't let the door bisect your firm arse on the way out.'

The man stood. 'You're making a disastrous mistake, Mr Mayor.'

'It won't be my first disastrous mistake. Nor my last. Good day.'

When the man was gone, the Mayor buzzed for his campaign manager, the lawyer Max Gaffer.

'What do you know about a man called Barny Juno?'

Gaffer added statute to his water and spoke as it dissolved. 'I think he's the one who held an illegal funeral and then pulled his trousers down. Bit simple-minded. They say he keeps eight hundred eels in his garden.'

'Has any of this been substantiated?'

'Everyone knows it. Jumping counters and pissing on arable land. Skimming manhole covers at old women. Some people are just basically rotten.'

'A simple "No" would have sufficed. What else?'

'Lives in that lopsided wooden thing on stilts. Near the chef school.'

'Looks like a giant chicken coop?'

'More like a gormless young man with your downfall on his mind.' Gaffer drained the glass. 'In the Coum district. Shacked up with about ninety animals. Or maybe a hundred. Around fifty per cent of them dangerous.'

'If there's a hundred, that'd make fifty of them dangerous, right?'

'I'm having a hard time following what you're trying to tell me, Mayor. Try pushing your lips out more.'

'I'm pushing my lips way beyond the boundary of good taste already. It's up to you to make it work for you. And where's Erno? That mute bastard's meant to sweep the building for floor lobsters first thing in the morning. I had to interrupt a serious meeting just now to stop one – look at that.' The Mayor pointed at the splat of exploded meat and shell on the carpet.

'Your office; your subconscious. So what was the meeting?'

'Chap swanned in here getting all bonier-than-thou. Wanted to back us. Claimed he had the red ear of the devil. Said Juno was a campaign handle. Pitched a poster campaign. This from a guy whose head was basically an elephant skull with a trumpet for a nose.'

'Really?'

'Well I imagine so. He was wearing some kind of mask.'

'Beware dreams born of paper, Mayor. You've got the Conglomerate to think of. And I've got underwear to buy.'

'You paints your wagon, you takes your choice. Remind me. What is it which, after a passage of time, leads us to question whether our colleagues are cruel or just stupid?'

'Their ignored advice.'

'That's right.'

'So are you counting the mask man a friend of yours?'

A shop with its own weather, the Thousand Spiders was a place of gut-turning symmetries and the slap of palpable etheric manipulation. In fact it was impossible to tell whether you really wanted to buy what you bought there. Barny, Edgy and Gregor moved between betsy lamps, puff-well traaasers, Spitain boxes, gas radios, galore sticks, vesta powder, canned stone, titan blades, carnival skins, scarcar spares, tree teeth, blackout cakes, cigars and dynamine mirrors. 'What's the big deal?' Gregor was saying irritably, looking at a punnet of pain spores. 'Of course I didn't want to be stuck there the whole night. I'd like to see you try.'

'Oh I get it,' said Edgy. 'Wham bam and you're outta there. Don't you value the closeness afterward, snuggling up? Aren't you interested in what's inside someone's head?'

'Closeness? There was a dead rat in there. How much closer could I get? *I* was the biggest thing inside her head. *Me.*'

'The ego on the guy. Eh Bubba?'

'I don't know, Edgy.' Barny was examining a small tin pyramid. 'Should I get one of these?'

'I'll tell you, me and Gort aren't afraid of affection. What about you and Red Alert? You snuggle up afterwards, right Bubba?'

'Well to tell you the truth Edgy, Magenta's sort of difficult to relax with.' In fact she made him feel like a bomb disposal expert. Just because he kept a few snakes and what have you, Magenta had pegged him as a roaring boy right off the bat and was furiously resistant to the barrage of contrary evidence. This extended mismatch was wearing him down but he was too placid to break it off. What a mess. He was less and less willing to lay amid this duplicitous construction. 'She's a real sparkplug.'

'For example.'

'Well, even her windchimes play nosebleed techno. Says it helps her sleep. She's so strong and vivid, Plantin, what can I say? She is beautiful.'

'She'll bring out the worst in you Bubba. You ready to learn that?'

'Yeah,' Gregor pitched in. 'Then bury you with a heart-shaped shovel.'

'Yeah well at least he doesn't sleep with animals who've already been buried for millions of years, dinosaur boy. You may be a sporting genius but that doesn't exempt you from the rules of society. I had to dance with a reptile to distract the community from what you did. Its scales were like dark jewels. I was in tears, Round One. *Tears*.'

'Can we change the subject please?' Gregor shouted. They all looked aside at the proprietor, an utterly rigid goat which, like all goats, dared one and all to believe it was made of timber. Dust was in her fur and darkness at her feet. She hadn't moved.

'Put down the Spitain, Bubba. It isn't good for what we have in mind. We need a Vanta grid like the one you were looking at that time GI Bill attacked us out of the blue.'

'Why again do you honestly believe you know so much about this stuff?' Gregor demanded.

'I *know* I know. Beltane Carom's a friend of mine, and he's the real thing. In fact he calls this a Mickey Mouse operation.'

'Well that fills us all with confidence – eh Barny?'

'I don't know, Round One. So why can't I use a box for the job, Edgy?'

'A Spitain works a certain way, Bubba. Hooks into the overlap of two warring entities, using the point of distraction as a weakness. Silent equivalents are born in the box which draw in the real thing like an anchor. So they're inside fighting like scorpions in a bottle. That's what keeps them in there.'

'What about a betsy?'

'Listen, a modern betsy lamp's basically just a palladium cathode in ectoplasmic suspension. It's like using a lava lamp as a headstone.'

'You know I can see auras, Edgy,' said Gregor in a contained sort of way. 'And yours is a bullshit borealis.'

Edgy picked up a thing like a collapsible kitchen trivet. 'That's the snare for the job, Bubba. Hey that reminds me, I'm gunna need some extra muscle stealing a cannon from the church later on.'

'Why,' squeaked Gregor, 'the *hell* do you need a church cannon?'

'Because Neville Peth's a member of the Patently Damaging Sports Club and he was distinctly unimpressed by my risk-taking the other night – thanks to you and your depravities, Round One. So anyway I'm planning to put on a little display for him and I need the cannon. Now Bubba, you owe me for taking the dog book off your hands.'

'I didn't ask for that, it's nothing to do with me.'

'Well listen I've already made some progress on it. I'm organising the whole thing under chapter headings. Dogs With Eager Faces, Dogs Who Are Warm to the Touch, Vertically Bounding Dogs, Dogs as Big as Me, Dogs in Cardigans, Enigmatic Dogs, Dogs Who Know My Name, Dogs Who Grudgingly Obey, Dogs of Neon, Dogs in a Pond, Dogs Who Gaze Into Infinity, Spent Dogs and like that.'

'Is this the book with the oil painting of you and the Alsatian?' Gregor asked.

'Yeah but the publishers, they're re-thinking the title. They're considering something along the lines of *My Dog Hell*. It's a marketing ploy. So listen Bubba, what about stealing the cannon?'

'I can't tonight, I'm seeing the Blaze. Ask Fang, he's a big man.'

'He's a *bog* man.'

Barny turfed through some weirdware. 'Think I should get something for the Blaze?'

'Everything comes with a reason not to do it,' muttered Gregor, examining a hex barb.

'Maybe you should pay more attention to those reasons, Round One,' Edgy murmured. 'You know GI Bill wants to kill you for what you pulled at the ballgame?'

'Kill me. He said that?'

'Well he used the word "destroy", but a man like that says more with his gestures. There were chopping motions, and he strangled the air. I think he'll leave some remains.'

Barny selected a small gas radio. 'All right can one of you guys take this up to the counter?'

'Don't tell me you're afraid of the goat. The little boy takes care of the punters.'

Through the sour, icy breeze from the darkling wormhole at the rear of the stockroom, waddled the kid Barny called 'Spooky Staring Boy'.

'I always forget there's a creeper exit back there,' Gregor said to himself.

'It's the boy I'm scared of,' whispered Barny, ducking. 'He never says anything. He stares at me.'

The kid would serve in silence and, at the last minute, murmur something which gave everyone the heeby-jeebies. This time they got as far as the door when, behind them, they heard the flat voice say: 'To pull up the soil and find blood.'

The way he welcomed the demon into his home, it was clear doomed Eddie Gallo was a mild man who persevered. To Dietrich's eyes he was little more than a cardigan with lips. On the wall were antlered potatoes. The demon laid out the campaign notion and the candidate made coffee. 'Siddown Mr Hammer. I hope five hundred rich tea biscuits aren't too many for you.'

'Thank you.'

'I see you've a copy of *The Stare*. Yes, Juno's attack on that useless fossil was pretty goofy if I say so myself.' He chuckled. 'Mind out for the piece of living death on the carpet there Mr Hammer. Now. I know Barny Juno. I stood up for him in court that time he pulled his pants down at the funeral. He's a nice man. Turns out I was stood in the dock stark bollock naked. These days frankly I don't dress unless I have to announce something to the town. And since I'm not an elected official and never have been, it almost never happens. Except I suppose in the courtroom, and I forgot that time. Everyone seemed to understand.'

'I see. I see. So. What's your electoral gameplan?'

'Well, there are some barely mobile sloths on the flyover. I'd like to raise people's awareness of their attitudes.'

'These are the brutes that block the road and explode when people get near them?'

'Yes, they basically prevent travel in that direction. Then after making a few damaging admissions I'll probably base everything around a general slogan. "A smile makes people wonder", something like that. It always goes that way. You know, I could give you a special balm for them saggy jowls, Mr Hammer.'

'Don't you think Barny Juno's been waiting for a way to show his gratitude? For your appearance in court? He'd love to give you a leg-up to the mayoral office. And my master can fund the entire sick jamboree. Remember what Violaine said about the fruitful thing?'

'The fruitful thing is true.' Doomed Eddie Gallo took a thoughtful snap from a biscuit. 'And Juno really wants to help me? He agrees to this? I suppose this is how it's done, isn't it? When can you start?'

Hammerwire stood, raised an arm and unfurled one white claw toward the centre of town. 'Now.'

It's impossible to excel at table manners – you conform to the pattern and extend no further, without expressiveness. Barny was ignorant of this – he only knew there was more oil on the table than in the vomit of a whale. 'It's everywhere,' he protested, looking at his hands.

'It's meant to be that way,' said Magenta Blaze. 'You're joking, right? It's vinaigrette for the salad.'

'This meal should be given a decent burial Madge, look at it.'

'You're hilarious.'

'I'm not,' Barny protested, 'no, I'm serious – we've been served a meal that's got all the hallmarks of sports turf. Look at it – it's arbitrary. What do they teach in that chef school?'

'Give it to the 'gator,' Magenta laughed, her big red mouth eclipsing her face. The reptile was under the table, sated with steak. The management of the Ultimatum Restaurant thought long skirts on the tables gave the place a sense of mystery, refusing to acknowledge that such a sense was supplied by the food.

'I got something for you,' said Barny wearily, producing the present.

'What is it? Stone make-up?' She unwrapped the gas radio, a natural gadget extruded from demon-blown amber which transmitted metallic whistling from the upper pain spectrum. 'Well. Wow.'

'Listen, Madge,' said Barny, as a strange mariachi band strolled up and began assailing their table. Magenta held the radio to her ear. 'I know you want to believe I'm some kind of wild man or something. And maybe I let you believe it at first. But the fact is, I don't really mean anyone any harm. Never have. I'm really a very boring person. I'm no threat to anyone. I just want to care for the winged and stepping animals of the earth, and be happy. So I think maybe we should just forget the whole thing.'

The band finished with a cry, throwing their sombreros at the ceiling.

'Did you say something, zeppelin?' said Magenta, taking the radio from her ear and squinting forward.

'Yes, Christ Almighty, I was saying I wouldn't harm a fly. Not the big ones anyway.'

Blaze laughed. 'Tell it to the trolls, baby. And pay the band.'

'All right I'll pay 'em.' Barny reached into his pants pocket for change and at that moment the 'gator launched out of its hiding place and clamped through the lead guitar in an explosion of twanging splinters. The guitarist screamed as if it were part of his body – which is the sign of a good musician.

'Let's go,' said Barny and went to snuff the candle flame between his fingers – soaked in oil, his hand caught fire with a sound like a jet ignition. He ran shrieking like a girl, setting fires around the establishment and finally punching his fist into a trifle.

It's a sad fact that most of their dates ended with them gazing out on a smashed landscape of slow flames, harking to the call and response of fire hydrants. The radio was the weirdest gift he'd ever given her. All she could hear on it was a sibilant voice saying 'Now' over and over.

As they led the reptile from the burning restaurant, the creature seemed to give a snapping yawn. The night walls, freaked with orange light, were plastered with campaign posters. Blaze was stumbling with laughter. 'When you said you'd pay the band, then reached down and set the 'gator on 'em? Then lit all those fires? You are the *man*, Bubba!'

'Magenta, you don't under*stand*.'

The posters they were passing bore the image of a scorched, fanged mantis with eyes like golf balls. Slogans varied from I SUPPORT DOOMED EDDIE GALLO IN HIS FIGHT AGAINST HAZARDOUS BARNY, through the quirky 800 EELS? 800 TOO MANY to the merely suggestive BARNY JUNO MUST BE 'DISPOSED OF' SOON. But these were topped out by the absolutist BARNY IS THE MOST DANGEROUS MAN IN THE WORLD. Magenta Blaze stood in front of this one as if it were unassailable holy writ.

Even Barny was able to detect the factor common to them all. They had all appeared sometime in the last hour.

It's amazing how a couple of thousand hostile posters in a two-mile area can mess with a person's progress. A baying mob's the thing to prevent a man from making plans and thinking of the future. The following day as Barny walked under a sky of cardiac blue, he drew the attention of a few sightseers who had been drinking official bile and gazing up at the Tower of Nowt. It was rumoured you could glimpse the moral fibre if you peered from a certain spot and this had become a site for stands selling hazardous snacks embossed with a worthless, treasured insignia. Barny's blank face was all the proof they needed. Their mouths advanced like car grills through street steam. And as Barny stood with the lightest curious frown, they inflated their lungs and banged out a volley of accusations at the region of his head: Sideburns on his legs. Overcast with hunger. Conceived in cola sex. Nailing behatted chicken heads to the doors. Wearing translucent pants. Secretly eats kebabs. Inflammation of the soul. Ignition socket instead of a knob. Summoned pig servant. Stood in fire, war typhoons shrieking out of his ears. Caused a house blast which shattered the exit ramp. Cast a squirmy package into the lake. Combs his spine with a wire brush. Wears a fish-head on his nose. Likeable as a chimp in an opera cloak. Risky as a dog in a chopper. Eight hundred eels. Dirty care and sax clubs. Alcohol twists his words. End of the sixpack, end of the world. Cheap with burning. Exhausted and wanton. Kidneys of stone. Flyaway sanity. Death grin. Code suit. Bollard hat, and so on.

As squalls of fresh slander were gathering, Barny made a mistake. Spotting a Gubba Man standing a short way off, he went over. These flesh statues were completely inanimate until someone approached them for help – then they would grab the poor sap and hold him in place with an iron grip. Some people starved to death in their clutches; some went mad. Others, prevented from escaping their pursuers, were left tilting bloody and deceased from the strong arm of the Gubba. Nobody really knew if the things were alive or contained anything more sentient than a one-way reflex mechanism. It was Barny's alarm and confusion which propelled him toward this vegetable sentry, and as the thick hand closed on his upper arm, he realised he'd got himself snared. Flooded with panic, he knew what it must feel like for the winged and stepping animals of the earth, cornered by chinless wonders. He scrabbled frantically at his restraint as the mob advanced.

Barny was spun to the ground. Feeling spaced out, he saw that the Gubba man's arm was still attached to his own. The crowd was screaming as the Gubba stood like a stone image, lacking a limb. Brought by Sid to meet Barny, the 'gator had flexed at the sentry, biting it through at the shoulder. The stump showed no detail, white as double cream.

People wandered frowning and puck-lipped out of bars. Neighbours aimed handheld cats at the commotion,. No matter how long it went on, nobody could ever get used to the electoral process.

5

Midnight, Unsuccessful

Any fool can last long enough to command respect

There was a little fuse chapel near the courthouse seeding lot. It was like a garage, the big door opening on to a short symbolic runway. A mid-sized black sternchaser faced away from the altar. Edgy and Gregor walked around the cannon, shining torches. Gregor was restless. 'Why do we spend our lives breaking into places at night?'

'Well that's a matter for the authorities, Round One. Right now we've got a job to do.'

'Shouldn't we be wearing some sort of black clobber for this?'

'I'm okay. Remember what old Bingo said? "Beauty, like nature, is unapologetic." I mean it.'

'White pants and a Hawaiian shirt? What's wrong with you?'

'Take a look at this altar, Round One.' Edgy ran the flash over streamer rolls, astrolabes, ready reckoners and target badges.

'It stinks in here.'

'Gunpowder. They call it "the lint of a joyous life". Get the bung and the hardhat, in the corner there.'

'Aren't these cannon places meant to be some kind of frenzied riot?'

'That's the Powderhouse, the fuse cathedral. This here's just a funeral unit. See this? Velocity Gospel, open at the rites. "Look out now, look out, look out, I'm lighting the fuse. There's gunna be one hell of a bang. Run, run." These guys crack me up.' Edgy went to check out the cannon.

Gregor frowned down at the heavy volume. '"Look at him/her go. Quick, say bye." Are these people serious?'

'They couldn't be more serious,' said Edgy, kneeling to examine the cannon wheels. He pulled out the blocks, tossing them aside. 'The uncertainty of ascension, wiped out in a single initiative. Put 'em into orbit. And they really laugh it up, I saw a segment about it on the Douglas Bar Show. They say the average fusehead writhes his body and contorts his face one hundred and fifty-three times a night. It's a bacchanalia round there at the Powderhouse – flaming torches, silver body paint, tumbling midgets, grapes. They go the whole hog. Help me with this, Round One.'

They shoved at the cannon, pushing it incrementally out of the chapel and toward the goods truck they'd borrowed from Mike Abblatia.

An hour later they were across the street from Neville Peth's house in a quiet cul-de-sac. All the house lights were out. Gregor stood on the flatbed next to the cannon, which was pointed at Neville's front window. Head and shoulders projecting from the cannon mouth, Edgy strapped on the hardhat, grinned and gave Gregor the thumbs-up.

'Why couldn't Barny do this?' Gregor asked wearily.

'Now you ask? He's busy, it's his dad's birthday. So let's spark up this bad boy.'

Gregor lit the fuse and Edgy yelled toward Peth's house. 'Hey Neville, check it out!' Almost instantly the cannon discharged, baulking backward through the truck cab. Gregor was on the ground, totally deaf, the look of disinterest frozen on his face.

Lights were beginning to flick on in houses. Wearing pyjamas, Neville Peth appeared in his doorway, peering toward the burning truck. After a little while he went back inside. The lights went off.

Gregor scrabbled up and climbed on to the flaming flatbed. Whisping with smoke, the cannon mouth was empty.

*

Through Accomplice passed a train which had no insides and was as full and solid as a stone. Fog and cobwebs billowed over the grey walls and nothing came out of the filled-in funnel. The driver was a statue obliterated in wall-to-wall marble. The train was born out of suffocation, went from nowhere to nowhere and appeared only at night. Barny didn't realise it was supposed to be scary and travelled on the roof when visiting his folks.

Springing off just after Jericho Bridge, he rolled through the mire and thumped to a stop against a rotten log. After staggering through the soupy swamp for an hour, he stepped through the warped door of the shack.

'Well, look who it isn't.'

'Happy birthday, father. Hello, mother.' Barny kissed the top of his mother's head. 'Hello, Ramone.' Barny opened the birdcage and kissed the moth in similar fashion. It was inured to this routine and lowered its head to receive the benediction.

'Did you bring a paper?' Ma Juno asked from her concrete chair. 'This one's ten days old.'

'I don't think anything of interest has happened, mother.'

'No paper? You know we rely on visitors out here. Henry, what kind of a son did you raise?'

'He's your son, Ethel.'

'Here's your present, father. And many happy returns.'

Pa Juno tore off the wrap and shop wadding, revealing the Vanta grid. 'A trivet? For holding a saucepan?'

'What do you buy the man who ate everything?' sneered Ma Juno.

'It's a snare for catching ghosts, father.'

Pa Juno looked wary and evasive. 'So? Well why give it to me?'

'Everyone knows your hairline's extended beyond your body, father – what were you going to do?'

'My long-standing policy is to ignore all creepy phenomenon and, if anyone mentions it, to quietly make the sort of face you'd see on the side of a church. Let 'em interpret it any way they want.'

'He just wants to pretend he's not as bald,' muttered Ma Juno, 'as a stone.'

'Maybe I've chosen to tuck my hair under my headskin to keep it dry in the summer storms. Did you ever consider that? I'm going to fish – and I don't care if it kills me.'

'Go fish then.'

'There's nothing fierce enough to be worth the catching.'

A chill stream of ghost-smoke flowed across the rear wall, blasting ornaments off the mantel. Barny's father stared pointedly the other way.

'Let's set it up then eh father?'

'You make this gizmo yourself? You using your welding skills?'

'Why would your son ever weld anything?'

'We sent him to welding school didn't we? You never know when you're gonna need to weld something together. Any number of social situations could arise. And he's your son.'

'I bought it, father.'

'Shop of a Cool Thousand?'

'A Thousand Spiders, father.'

'There – your son's been dabbling in the dark arts after all, Ethel. Didn't I say he'd hit the headlines for crimes against nature?'

'A good father should give his son a chance, Henry. You know we need etheric insulation. We can't be here inhaling ghosts. Sharp on the throat. Mankind is meat – nature's in league with the stones.'

'So Edgy says it works like flypaper,' Barny continued, placing the grid at the centre of the floor. 'You know that stuff in the tub, in the Shop? Golem fat or whatever it's called. Ecto stuff for building creatures. And E.H. Hunt – you know, who carries that huge chest around for some reason? Gregor says he was in the Shop, Hunt was, and he was laughing about something or other, and so much his false teeth flupped out into the vat and a travertine demon started growing there. The mix had to be incinerated but Hunt was made to pay anyway.'

'You're the worst storyteller I ever heard,' said Ma Juno.

'No son of mine could relate the facts so badly. And no paper!'

'Well, so Edgy told me this works a bit like that, but he says as an anchoring tool. It weaves this membrane between the spokes, which is a really thin flesh bed doped with charged ecto stuff. So the ghost gets drawn to it and stuck? Then you can put it on like a crown, father, and hey presto.'

The dark forces were activated by placing the grid on a clammy pasta base, which Barny had brought in some foil. Within a few moments a misty cobweb developed across the little 2-D cage. Then a few fibres appeared, wisping like fungal spores. Black hair was sprouting, a puppet's moptop. Something semi-visible was pouring into the grid.

'What's this?' asked Ma Juno. She was looking at some scrunched padding from Barny's gift. It was a piece of newspaper which she was flattening out. 'Lard-arse born from fossil? "Barny Juno took the biscuit yesterday by sprouting a living potato man from the skull of an ancient monster. When asked to comment, he said 'I don't understand.'" Your father was right. Crimes against nature. What did you do, create some kind of pig servant?'

'It's not a pig servant, it's Gregor. He was trapped in the fossil.'

'Ethel, look at this – my hair.' There was a great pool of hair filling the room out, writhing like snakes, reaching for the walls. Ma Juno started screeching. Chairs and side-tables were shoved by the flow. The hair pool became white at the heart, then stopped growing. The grid buzzed and spat like a frying hive. The room was full. 'It's all the hair I ever had in my life.'

Pa Juno skipped through the hair sea and picked up the grid, hauling the hair after like a wedding veil, and placed it on his head. The hair was alive, tentacular, roiling in thick ropes. Pa Juno laughed a gummy laugh, an overblown gorgon, a side-lamp freaking his shadow.

Barny backed into the dark wall, gripping his fear, and a whisper hissed through his head. *I've created a monster.*

6

Nothing is Revealed

Beneath tree birds, cats rise like watchtowers

Mayor Rudloe had ordered Erno to set up a Raj-style carpet fan in the big office and now there it was, slowly swinging with a dozen or so floor lobsters clinging to it. 'What is this,' said the Mayor, 'an amusement park for these animals? Shake 'em off, you silent bastard.'

Erno, drawing slow on the rope, looked at him mournfully.

Max Gaffer shot into the room with a copy of the *Stare*. 'Looka this, Mayor.'

'I'm working up a speech for Parade day. It's all about my jaws, and how the hinges work. It's dynamite.'

'Mayor, listen to this. "BARNY JUNO'S PIG SERVANT STEALS FROM CHURCH. A vat-grown mutant potato creature hatched by Barny Juno from the skull of a dead beast has stolen a sacred cannon from a fuse chapel and set fire to it in the suburbs. Opposition mayoral candidate doomed Eddie Gallo, whose campaign is centred around the condemnation of Juno, baffled the media by commenting: 'I know Barny Juno. I like him a lot. He takes care of animals in his funny house. I'm sure his pig servant had the best of intentions.' Rod Jayrod, Fusemaster of the Cannon Sect, stated: 'This is not the first deliberate sacrilege perpetrated by this man against cannonic scripture. The bastard planted a dead lizard one time, then while he was pretending to cry, he showed his arse to the whole world. That was a day for eyelids.' Barny Juno, who also uses the alias Juniper, is known to own an eight-foot alligator which means business and will kill us all." Then there's a picture from the lizard funeral – looka that.'

'Get that thing away from me! How did this happen? If every man were as static as doomed Eddie Gallo nothing in the world would need a word of explanation. I ever tell you the first time I saw him? He was wandering in traffic with a maple branch. How did a man like that recognise this Juno trump card?'

'He makes it look so easy.'

'He's probably having a good laugh about it right now. Anyway an alligator? Any animal that blinks sideways has gotta have some strange ideas. If it, say, grips a fella with them teeth and makes him perish in a messy sort of way, screams and what have you? What about it?'

Max Gaffer smirked. 'I can see his cavalier leading of a reptile around town could be a disaster for the Accomplice community.'

'You'd cordon off the rain, wouldn't you?'

'It's not enough to believe in ourselves, Mayor – we gotta curse everyone else.'

'That why I'm going out kissing babies?'

'I think we should hold back on the doorstepping, Mayor. The old bag's suing about her fish.'

'That guppy was ceramic! She put it in my hands like an infant!'

'Well she was upset in any case, and the stills of her bent sobbing over the pieces are quite appallingly damaging. You standing there awkward, uncomprehending and all? I tried to buy her off but the crazy bird wanted to handle my underwear. She's a tough nut to crack.'

'You're sure about the underwear? She said this?'

'Well, I got a sense of it.'

'So once again you wreck everything through your belief that everyone's preoccupied with your underwear.'

'You want I should send the Brigade in?'

'Boy, yours is a lofty profession Max. Lucky for men like me. However far we ascend in office, we never reach those heights where the law dwells.' A floor lobster fell on to the desk and both men recoiled. A whiplike antenna nearly had the Mayor's eye out. 'Christ almighty! Erno, have you heard a bloody word I've said? Put these megabugs in the furnace!'

Erno stopped tugging the pulley and grudgingly got a broom, knocking the giant insects off the fan.

'I want a mailshot,' the Mayor continued. 'The mask man kept going on about the 'gator. Focus on it in the fliers. "Fatal to you, fatal to me", like that. I think it's valuable – offer a reward which we won't give. A mass mailing. Every household in Accomplice. We'll tell them I'm the man to act against the antisocial element and croak it on a personal basis. If the reptile's a dud we sell it to Karloff's Circus. I want them in the mail today. There's nothing to stop us.'

In the stale half-light of the sorting office, B.B. Henrietta considered giving the walls a haircut. Toads surfaced smiling in the watercooler. Sags Dumbar looked glum and doubtful.

In the past everyone had feared Dumbar because his head was actually a chrysalis for another animal. In recent times his face had been almost transparent and they could see something bustle and shift behind it. Finally he'd stopped short in the middle of a conversation and opened his mouth, from which a bunch of fiddling spider legs fanned. Everything else followed and he was speechless and shaking, the only one without a scream to offer as the dog-sized bug quivered into a corner and stayed there to dry off. But he was a steady worker.

The huge bug was kept in a lobster cage in the back of the basement and only Barny was preoccupied enough to approach and feed it some giblets. So why they should be bothered by an alligator is anyone's guess.

'Why do the papers keep calling me a pig servant?' asked Gregor, climbing up from his room in the little sub-basement. It was grim accommodation but maybe he was better off than Fang, who as one of the living dead was obliged to go and bury himself in the marshes and keep his gob shut.

'You can be anything you want to be, fatboy,' Edgy assured him.

'What? Don't call me that. What?'

Barny had told them how public hostility had manifested itself in the swerving noses of passers-by, whispers, multi-legged attacks and so on. But everyone was more interested in Edgy's adventure.

'I guess when the cannon went off,' Edgy explained, 'I decided at some subconscious level to respond with a kind of flying-through-the-air-and-screaming gambit, sideways through the sky, higher than I'd planned.'

'What then?' asked Barny.

'Well I followed that up with a simple landing gambit.'

'You continued with the screaming?'

'For the moment. Of course I tailed that off eventually and found myself lying face down in spongy sand and utter darkness. My whole nerve rig was firing. The place was thick with clams. Huge tidal silences, Bubba. Leaking rock pools. Fossil bombs. At midnight, I might add. And you know who I saw there? The Announcement Horse. He was perched there like Napoleon, gazing out. He made a few cracks about me.'

'Cracks?'

'Ah, you know how he is – said I was doomed etc. Burnt paper over my bones, a window made of light, jellyface colleagues with all the backbone of pizza. What else . . . stuff about the community generally, phone-faced killers, several brawls of no great consequence, a few moonlit riots, beware the chair, one man two names, sores of beauty. Said only a puzzle with defined edges can be solved. What a card.'

'Beware the chair. He's a funny guy.'

'And made completely of metal, I know that now. I'm telling you Bubba, it's a long while since I visited the old baffling ocean. We should all go a lot more.'

B.B. Henrietta pitched in. 'That guy Hunt goes on about it so much, why bother?'

'B.B., remember what old Bingo said? Joy is whatever you approach individually, without duty, coercion or clouded mind. That's what happened to me on the beach, people. But at top speed.' Edgy described little bony triangular shells and how the succulent roots fanned out, whipping velveteen husks and polished pupils. They had seemed so weird with their limbs out, a sappy predator for the warm mud, gradually revealed.

'You're not converting to Velocity are you?'

'Oh not me. Or the doll house neither. None of it's real to me. And why would something that's everywhere need a window?'

'Yeah I saw on Douglas Bar how all kinds of people used to have god harassing them, giving them advice,' said Fang.

'Oh I heard the voice of god once,' Edgy told him. 'Yeah, I was at a buffet, you know? And I was going for the chicken, and this voice from above said, "Take the ham." So that's what I did.'

'Take the ham. And that's the only time god ever chose to give you advice.'

'Correct. I can only conclude that in every other area of my life I've been right on the money.'

'So what did Mike Abblatia say about the truck?'

'Nothing. He'll forgive anything. The man's unnatural. Anyway, I'll have to impress Neville Peth some other way – he's a cool customer.'

'All right I've heard enough,' said B.B. Henrietta, returning to her work. She was squashing a package of brittle-sounding stuff as small as possible, to throw into the bushes later. The slightest jog of the sorting table sprayed salty tears everywhere.

At that moment an explosion of boxes banged down the chute, tailgaiting each other on to the conveyor – forty of them. The silence afterward was broken by a fatalistic groan from B.B. Henrietta, who lugged one of the boxes over. Someone had to make a start. Slitting it open, she removed a paper pocket, which she tore to reveal a printed leaflet which said that Barny's alligator was unpredictable. 'All these boxes? What are they doing here?'

Fang, his face a dried, dented fruit, touched the package

gingerly. 'All right. I'll tell you what we're gonna do. In the Drop, all of them. There's no room for half measures.'

'No, there's too much stuff,' Gregor snapped, gripping Fang's arm – it drifted away in his hands, water and some black fluid trickling from the shoulder stump. Dropping the limb, Gregor backed up and shrieked in a demented sort of way, his face twisting like a corkscrew.

'There's no time,' shouted Edgy. 'It's three o'clock already. Into the Drop.' He speared a bundle and pitched it into the maw.

But Gregor's protest was well founded. Apparently bottomless as a skeleton, the Drop made terrifying noises if more than one ton of stuff was dumped at a time. The boxes reached this threshold in a few minutes and the Drop maw started bellowing like a mammoth. Gregor rushed to the furnace and stuffed three boxes in there, clogging the door and tamping the pressure. Blasted by recoil and stumbling with flailing arms, he seemed a troll toiling against the ferocious oven. Hot coals spat and rolled on to the floor. Flame rampaged over furniture like the branding fire of shame. The crew were wading through charred mysteries, every step a deposit for death by worry and wasted time. Ashes drifted past the clockface. 'We can change, can't we?' said Fang, not really believing it. 'Step, step, all smiles. Bam we're in a new location, springing.' And he choked suddenly, folding down into sobs. Coughing in a fog of swirling cinders, Barny blasted Dumbar's bubbling face with a fire hydrant.

Edgy was saying, 'For god's sake stretch my nose to the door and sod the expense!' when the Captain descended carrying a hazardous freight of disinterest.

'Now then lads,' he said, regarding the unlivable hell of smoke and embers, 'simmer down. Some things don't escape me: Barny. It's come to my attention. How shall I put it. It's come to my attention that you have some kind of public feud going on with the devil.'

'Doesn't everyone?' asked Edgy mildly, and tossed a suave grin at the others.

'Or an apparition along similar nerve-jangling lines. It's on posters all over town, saying it's backing doomed Eddie Gallo in his campaign against your hot-damn depravity.'

'One day you'll understand me better,' said Barny, squinting through the foul air with bloodshot eyes.

'Well that's as maybe, but gee wizz I cannot allow my employees to be menaced by a bleak demon, fire hosing out its nose and so on.'

'Attaboy,' nodded Edgy.

'And as for an angry mob. Unacceptable.'

'Outstanding.'

'So I'm going to have to let you go, Barny.'

'What?' Edgy spluttered. 'You can't. He's got eight hundred eels to take care of. As everybody knows.'

'I'll have the roast beef platter,' said Sags Dumbar, his placental head sagging on to his shoulder.

'And get me a shrimp cocktail,' Barny piped brightly. 'What's the matter?'

'He's firing you, Bubba.'

'Firing me . . .' Barny's slow bewilderment was perfectly apparent.

'Someone set him up,' said Edgy.

'You have enemies?' the Captain asked Barny.

'He's got thousands. Ask, I mean, ask around. Bubba here's hit the jackpot as far as nemeses are concerned. He's unspeakably offensive. Tell him, Bubba.'

'A person can only have one nemesis,' stated the Captain wearily. 'That's the nature of a nemesis.'

'The nature of a nemesis eh. Listen to the expert.'

'And in regard to *your* conduct in this matter, Gregor. We all know you as a bloated fool who tries and tries. I confess until I read the headlines today I didn't realise you were Barny's pig servant – now I see that by golly you've never been fully responsible for your own actions. Church theft and vandalism reflects badly upon this industry and I answer to Mr Gibbon. However, I'm told you have a legitimate statue in the Garden and so I intend to intercede on your behalf. It's known that a simple exorcism procedure followed by counselling can make an ectomorphic mutant like yourself a passably productive member of society. Here's Doctor Perfect's number, call him today. Give a good account of yourself in public and after some passage of time we'll review the situation. One chance, Gregor. Behave.'

'Ectomorphic mutant?' Gregor gasped.

'And as for the rest of you—' snapped the Captain, and trotted up the stairs, slamming out.

'I wish he wouldn't do that,' muttered Fang.

'Out of the frying pan and straight to video, eh Round One?' said B.B. Henrietta.

Edgy watched Barny with concern.

'Don't worry about the Captain,' said Fang, draping his arm around Barny's shoulder and walking away. 'Pound for pound he's more of a ponce than anyone.'

A half-hour later, Barny wandered dazed from the office and stood in the street like a fool newly made.

High above him hovered the demon Dietrich, like a coat thrown into the sky.

7

Pantomime Horse

Never use your eyeball as a paint roller

Laughing as the lion licked eight layers of skin from his face, Barny shoved him away and got a steak out of the oven. 'Body temp,' he said, prodding it with a thermometer, and flapped the bloody meat toward the cat. He gestured at his gruesome generator. 'Thank god the place is powered on dung. But what about food and supplies? I need reptile lights for Mister Newton, mice for the snakes, raisins for the mice, fruit for the chimps, gore for Mister Braintree here. I can't set him loose on the community like Karloff used to. Can I?'

Edgy rested on the lion's head. 'You need to find a new course of exhaustion, Bubba. I'll coach you. Del needs a tong man at the Foundry. Anyway he looks like he does. He's badly burnt. And we know Stampede Products have got at least one vacancy for the old door-to-door.'

Edgy said this because when Barny got back from being fired he found the alligator in the course of eating an alleged Stampede Products salesman. Golden Sid clung screaming from a light fitting as the 'gator thrashed the furniture to pieces and the visitor's screams merged with his own. Barny noticed a target badge on the stranger's chest as the reptile chugged him back. Phoning the Powderhouse he got only laughter and a heavy beat on the line. Barny would never understand that the salesman was in fact an assassin sent by the Powderhouse in retribution for the Mister Spiderman funeral. Ironically the man had been hyping damnation curtains, which were traditionally hung to signal to the neighbourhood that everything was going to hell inside.

Barny looked gloomy. 'Just when I get the 'gator settled in enough for Golden Sid to handle twice a week, it looks like I'm going to be here anyway. At least he won't need paying.'

'Do you get the full meaning yet re the 'gator? You see, your 'gator? Inscrutable. Enigmatic. It's got a way of posing totally still, not a flicker. That'll freak anyone out. Then it suddenly jolts into action. People have got a right to scream, Bubba. Can't you understand you're the only person in the world who thinks that monster needs protecting?'

'Isn't that the definition of love?'

'What?'

'Its legs are really quite delicate.'

'What? So?'

'So it's slow. Slower than a croc.'

'Listen to me Bubba, you've gotta do something about it. Everyone obviously hates it and they'll start to hate you. I've seen it happen.'

'How can they not adore it? It's got a head like a pike, you've seen its head.'

'Yes I've seen the head. But people judge by broad, general appearances and this 'gator of yours has the appearance of being a giant, toothsome reptile with the potential to throw a tantrum no matter what you say. Remember Joe Fuel?'

Edgy reminded Barny of the Prancer-organised campaign among the Accomplice community to stare, point and whisper regarding Joe Fuel's facial area, adding enigmatic phrases such as 'Not enough money to see to it?' over a period of years until Joe Fuel came to a gritty acceptance of what he was convinced were the most inconvenient cheeks in the world.

'So what?' asked Barny. 'What's that got to do with Mister Newton?'

'Appearances, Bubba. We'll dress it up as something else. A judge. A failure. A Portakabin. A little lamb. A ladle. A monster of some kind. The possibilities are, yes, limitless aren't they? See what I'm saying?'

'Or a gimble.'

'What's a gimble?'

'I don't know,' Barny confessed.

'Well, that's an okay place to start. The important thing is to be inconspicuous. Until inactivity is recognised as an expression of willpower, people will disregard it, that's what old Bingo said. These people are afraid you'll damage the moral fibre.'

'Why? I've never seen it. The only time I stood near the door of the Tower I had a really dodgy time with the guard guy Murdster.'

'What did he do?'

'Stepped forward and forward, hands raised and rounded like claws, and held my neck tightly, his teeth like a car radiator. I realised after a while that he meant to kill.'

In the acid night of Sweeney's cave, the demon looked through undulating blood at Barny's moonlike face as words echoed. 'I realised after a while that he meant to kill.'

'Look at those wide, vacant eyes,' said Sweeney. 'This is a man without the inconvenience of caution. I was correct in thinking he was only hex-protected against direct assault. The strange, ramped design of the house appears to incorporate several unfamiliar geomantic hypergrams.'

Using a dog's ribcage to comb the arterial tubing of his head, Dietrich glanced up at the Ruby Aspict. 'The scarecrow man in the bright shirt, the one who rests upon the lion's head. His name is Plantin Edge. He flirts with danger. This activity seems to serve as an entertainment for Juno.'

'A clown? Apprentice? Or a protector?'

'He boasts that his balls detach and fly away at night.'

'An apprentice then. A novice still impressed with parlour tricks. And what are these you've brought me? Headstones for moths?'

'Rich tea biscuits, Your Majesty. Some form of "gift" forced upon me by doomed Eddie Gallo.'

'Five hundred of the buggers. You seem to have made an

impression on the upper world, Dietrich, but don't let it go to your slick head. I won't have another desertion.'

Sweeney was making a wounded reference to the demon Gettysburg, who had defected to the upper world after popping out to buy some fags.

'Something's happening.' Dietrich's rock fissure eyes squinted at the Aspict – its rotation had begun to accelerate. 'I can feel corpse shoes creaking in chill hallways.'

'It's got a hook in them,' said the huge white beetle, leaning as far as his armoured throne allowed. 'Onrushing like a shark tag. Now we'll see some action.'

It seemed things were moving quickly. Baffled by the non-delivery of his leaflets, the Mayor had begun a specifically anti-alligator poster campaign. Barny and Edgy set upon an iffy course of camouflage. At first Barny thought it would suffice to add some length to the snout and a couple of false externally visible lower teeth, thus disguising the alligator as a crocodile. Staring pop-eyed at the carnivore, the inhabitants of a kebab shop ran screaming exactly as if it were an alligator, Barny running after them with a colour-coded jaw diagram. 'The teeth you bastards, the *teeth*!' The incident was held up as proof, if any were needed, of Barny's precocious evil.

The grey-green rocky monster seemed to work well as an old log until a cat tried to climb inside. As a sleeping tramp under a battered coat it regularly broke character to snap at charitable strangers in a thrash of incisors and hectic dust. Its appearance as a giant furled leaf was baffling to E.H. Hunt and they had to explain it to him just as if he were a child. His bafflement reached such a tortuous extreme he was blatantly relieved when it turned out to be a mere reptile. The rills on its back suggested to Edgy a rigid stage prop representing seawaves, so they painted the 'gator blue and stood pulling it awkwardly back and forth behind the actors in a production of Violaine's *Exhaustion Babe*. The audience were baffled, not least because the play was set in an urban wasteland and contained no reference to the sea. The entire effort was a waste of time.

Turning from these scenes in the Aspict, the demon Dietrich felt a tiny worm squirm in the wet clawhammer of his head. Was Barny Juno no more than an unbelievable moron?

Barny was trudging subdued through the square as Prancer Diego, founder of the high-speed run-up point-blank insult, stood yelling some towering truth to one and all. 'Hold up Bubba,' Prancer shouted, and came over.

Barny liked Prancer in a cautious way. The prankster shuddered and grinned a lot and blew industry-standard magnets out of his nose. When reversed baseball caps came back into fashion for a while he wore the bill forwards and had his head surgically reversed. He even questioned the bells of despair.

'Oh hi Dago,' said Barny.

'That monster of yours doesn't have much to recommend it, Juniper. Why not gut the thing and pump it up, make it a balloon? No? Well, don't say I never gave sound advice in times of peril.'

'I dunno Dago, everyone seems to hate me in an unfocused sort of way,' said Barny. 'Got me fired. I can't see why the 'gator can't participate in this community. They're always claiming that's the goal.'

'Charm can work when culture negatives other tricks. Watch this.' And Diego approached a small bright-eyed dog, which looked up at him eager. 'Use me, use me!' he shouted at the mammal, which reacted by yapping loud, skittering sideways. He strolled back to Barny, grinning with pride and high spirits. 'So you see? I'm correct.'

'You're a nice man, Dago,' said Barny. 'But you're not very good with the winged and stepping animals of the earth.'

'Everyone yelps when they've got a principle, Juniper, uncertain if it's a thorn or a medal.'

'I've got no idea what you're talking about.'

8

King Verbal

A patron is like a loving devil

Despite his protestations of harmlessness Barny had a tendency to eat small, struggling trolls when nervous. B.B. Henrietta sometimes shook him by the shoulders but apart from this he received no organised support toward kicking the habit. In fact her shaking him by the shoulders made him giggle like a child and he liked it. Barny carried a small troll in his briefcase as he entered the boneseed factory and ran through his answers in his head. Edgy had coached him with ruthless efficiency, grabbing him by the face and stretching his cheeks out in a desperate sort of way. Toward the end Edgy had shouted, 'Take it or leave it!' three times and begun sobbing with anger. Barny chased the alphabet with cloak flying, and resolved he was ready. King Verbal guided him into a plush office with gales of good humour. Radiating brisk, boundless energy, he directed Barny to a seat.

'Barny Juno. Thrilled to bits you came in. I will not, cannot believe, that a beekeeper's mask is necessary at an interview of this kind.'

'I opted for the formal.'

Verbal sat in a soft lurch chair. 'You'll find we're quite relaxed here Mr Juno. Coffee?'

'Bring it now.'

'Pop the mask off and put it here. That's right. Yes, I've looked at your application. I've had that honour and I must say your CV's an abomination.'

'Thanks. My friend Sags Dumbar's got a transparent head.'

'Really? Really. Well you saw my partner, King Fletch, through the broken door just now. King Perchant has a massive hernia and won't be joining us. He's the money man. My chief concern these days is quality control. It's a key issue with me. Efficiency has moved on immeasurably since the skeleton coast disaster. Look me in the eye and tell me you don't know about that. Sure you do, who doesn't? And as the founder of the boneseed process I was a key player in the mayhem that followed.' Verbal steepled his hands and looked aglow. 'I used to be a doctor. Along came some ill bastard and my medical career hit the fan. In this universe lungs are in a tiny minority. Minerals are where it's at Barny, get my drift?'

'Yes, ma'am.'

Verbal chuckled benignly. 'All right Barny, but when you get to my age you'll be regaling one and all with stories of your own achievements, and just looking at you I can sense your potential. You've got a big life ahead of you boy. So humour me a little further. See that map of Accomplice? The whole west side was open country back then. One day I was churning toxins with a handle when one of my many enemies attacked from behind, falling in after a brief struggle. I looked down into the tumult – I'd like to say his bones were reacting with the mix in a useful way, but frankly he was just floating there. However, that was the start of my life venture. Hardhat research, a trip to ancient trinkets and erosion, I waded in heavy. My big dream of an automatic building material able to spread from seed. Five years later my first boneseed complex was spreading like frost on a window, completely out of control as it turned out and clogging the entire west horizon. Boy, there's a day I won't forget in a hurry. Terror, screaming, people getting caught in the flow and bonding in for ever. Seventeen hours it took. I remember one in particular when a towerlike confusion of ribs locked upward into stairs, oh, no one could deny we'd arrived. As you can tell, I'm secretly proud of Accomplice's botched geology. The chaos of the coast is classic, behold. But in business nothing stands still. We've developed the shortlife mix which you've seen in the courthouse and other buildings. We're working with colour compounds for brighter striation, bird calcium for finer design – stand back and watch me dream of a brighter future. Yes sir there's a party in my arse and everyone's invited. And this is my challenge to you, Barny. How far can *you* obsess? What's your dream?'

'I want to care for the winged and stepping animals of the earth, and be happy.'

'Ah don't we all – that's a cop-out answer. I mean your fiercest dream Barny, something that grabs your gizzard and chokes it like a swan.'

Barny recalled Edgy's teachings. 'I want to be tormented by duty, Mr Verbal. Until I weep.'

'Well, strictly speaking, Barny, we don't like our employees to be tormented to that degree. But I admire your spirit. How was it in your last office? Good atmosphere?'

'Together we watched rats eat the clock. Decorated invisible bees with gifts. Dust everywhere. I have marmosets.'

'Is that so. Well you've seen the scope and grandeur of our operation, Barny. No floor lobsters on us, we see to it. We live by the first rule of business: garbage at crippling prices. As a Boneseed employee you'll run the gamut. Learn ugliness and groundless respect. Notorious pint initiation. A minimum of five hours a day in the bird room with bandaged shoulders. Despair the live-long year.'

Barny flipped the catch on his briefcase.

'So here's the bottom line, Barny. Why do I need you? What sets you apart from the mass of people?'

'A shrapnel scar on my spine the colour of banana talks to me at night, filling the room with whispers.'

Verbal frowned a moment. 'Well by god that's the best answer I ever heard. I want to hire you Barny – I know you must have other offers. If they insist, the only possible course is to shrivel and twirl, acting strange till they leave you alone. Kick those bastards into touch. You're made for life. Golden address and foreign guests, you'll never look back you rascal.'

'Caviar is murder.'

'Beg pardon? What's with the troll?'

'I can't put a stop to it.'

'Barny. Barny don't be doing that—'

Barny bit into the troll's belly, tearing out the blue guts.

Verbal bridled. 'Hey Juno a young man's personal chaos is terrible and bad I'll grant you – but that's a troll you're eating there. A real troll. I mean consider the science, look at me. Tell me you're hungry for challenge, boy, I can see it in your eyes . . .'

A dream seemed to settle over Barny's sated face.

'Don't blow it Barny it's right here—'

'I bite and bite them Mr Verbal.'

Verbal closed up, becoming grim. 'Don't mess with me Barny. I elbowed a chimp to get this far and I won't let you wreck it now.'

Of all life's instants, being ejected from a job interview one backward step at a time, each step provoked by a punch upside the face from the interviewer, is one tailor-made for grim reflection. Barny squandered this opportunity. The above scenario was repeated with only minor variations at a dozen offices that day, until the gored and purpling Barny approached the Shop of a Thousand Spiders. One half-minute late for the interview, he found the barred door closed upon him in the dimming light, Spooky Staring Boy standing utterly still beyond the threshold.

His last stop was Del's Fright Foundry, a psychodimensional vortex from which the gruff barrelman Del would drag horrific, steaming artifacts directly on to the street. Totally useless, these arcane masses would sit steaming in the public byway until the populace dared urge him to get them out of sight. 'Who said I need an assistant?'

'Edgy. He said you were getting badly burnt.'

'Do I look badly burnt?'

'Yes.'

'Come into the garage.'

Del had a garageful of massive insect skeletons which he'd brought through from another realm. Grey crablike things the size of cows. Great serrated saw-wavers. Buggy-whip antennae. Whiskered shells. Called it the Dark Armoury, and so it was.

You could all too easily picture these mothers ratcheting and alive – it was something to do with the dozens of legs and confounding detail. Played jumpy tricks on the eye. One bug, an armoured beast the size of a Volkswagon and which Del had christened 'Trouble', was exactly like one of those supermagnified carpetbugs from the wonders of science. Its roof was thin dry flaky leather. Del said there was next to no meat inside and that the brute lifted as light as an inflatable chair.

Upon introduction to these beasts, the scenario Barny feared was that one day Del would return to find that the position of one of the exhibits had subtlely changed. Del confirmed that this was a regular occurrence. Barny had visions of the creatures slamming into each other like dodgem cars the moment they were alone.

'If you work for me,' said Del, 'it will be your job to stay in here overnight and observe.'

'Well I'm sorry we couldn't do business, Del.'

They walked back out to the foundry mouth. Del picked up the massive tongs and plunged them into the flurrying vortex. 'Ask the sorcerer Beltane about those stupid posters.'

'He scares me.'

'You scare us all, lunatic. With your goddamn placidity.' This last was drowned out by gurgling birthcries as a snagged neck emerged black from the static.

9

Take a Deep Breath

Only a bastard tries to cauterise a wound with an account of his own past injuries

Fear the doctor who snorts in breeches and lives in a dungeon.

'Blame me for everything,' he whispered to himself in the scabby cavern of his surgery. Dirt fell from the bulbswing roof as the stone train roared overhead. 'We have only the turnip of conformity to fend off our demons. No wonder. And nobody hears my name. From here I can blame everybody.

'Monsters visit me here, banging me on the back and saying I've done well. Call me a "rascal" and expect me to respond. Why can't I be left alone to hammer these grail fragments to the wood backing? Freedom is tasteless, tell everyone.'

The marriage fanfare announced his entry into the toilet. 'By god, give me a nation and I'll stare blankly at you, whoever you claim to represent. Bloody my hands with your prestructured farm notions? Crop rotation? Just bake me something and get out of here.'

'Doctor Perfect?'

The doctor halted abruptly, realising he had been talking aloud. He emerged from the toilet, wiping his hands. 'Conscious of the floor are we?'

Doctor Perfect's brain was external, perching on his head like a gran's hairstyle. The brain was in a visibly bad state, yellow infections beating like a heart amid dockleaf veins and a peppering of skull lint. No one ever dared mention it.

Gregor approached his own betterment like a clown talking through a taut door chain. Confronted with this shambling grotesque, he stood fidgeting at his own aura. 'I didn't know you did head work, Doctor Perfect.'

'Why shouldn't I?' snapped the doctor. 'What kind of question is that? Just sit yourself on the smashed Daimler there. We'll tongue the planet in your head. Or you'll end up exploding naked into the streets, screaming and demented, semolina dripping from your beard.'

'I don't have a beard,' Gregor quailed, lying back on the banging roof of the crushed car.

'You will. Trust me. You know, the Captain's sticking his corded neck out for you. Front page news – PIG SERVANT STEALS FROM CHURCH. You must be terribly proud. You've got a head like a scallop bulb, you know that?'

'Yes.'

'Well that's a start. Health is part boredom and part repair.' Doctor Perfect sat on an upturned trashcan. 'I want to make it clear at the outset that I resent golem cases and I resent you. Between you and me this flimsy headcharge you call a life strategy is propelling you like billy-o toward your downfall in flames and trouble, explosions banging open right next to your ear. Just so you'll know. Not to mention the appalling expense. You were created by a co-worker a few days ago using a dinosaur head as a template, correct?'

'No.'

'Let me be the judge of that, laddie. Exomorphs can even be made by accident. You know Hunt? The guy who drags that chest everywhere—'

'I know, he dropped his false teeth in the vat.'

'You've heard that one?'

'I was there.'

'No, this was months ago.'

'I'm nobody's pig servant!' Gregor spat in strangled exasperation.

'That's the spirit. But the flesh is weak. Get any exercise?'

Gregor muttered something about a morning sprint combined with the punching of blurred strangers. He looked without much interest at the doctor's desk. Cobweb decanter, stiff raven and ancient wax puddle. There were several mannikins propped in the shadows. 'What's with all the dummies?'

'Oh, I have an interest in the statue problem round here. I'm not even sure it's a problem at all. I'm thinking of stealing a Gubba Man and seeing what's inside.'

'Barny broke one the other day – there's nothing inside but solid milk.'

'Oh, I doubt very much that he did,' said the doctor with a patronising smile. 'Ever heard of statue therapy, laddie? No? Might be just the thing for you. It's a matter of identity and esteem, you see. You go to Scardummy Garden. Find your statue. Pamper that abomination. Give it some nice threads. Decency anticipates investigation, but it's a start.'

Gregor whimpered with impatience. 'I can't ponce around in the Garden, it creeps me out. I don't have time, I have responsibilities. G.I. Bill says he'll destroy me for stealing the ballgame.'

'I doubt he used the word "destroy". G.I. Bill's a butterball with a few motor skills and that's all. But I accept that stupidity's crown presses upon you with its duties and obligations. Elderly folk to care for?'

'No. They used to live in the Swamp of Eternal Enmity/Degradation. Got sold some tin siding that gave the shack too much weight. It sank without trace.'

'How convenient. Without trace you say? And you still deny you're a pig servant. You're a sly bastard, eh?'

'Listen, I was in the dinosaur skull because I wanted to purge my lust. The guard came in. I had to hide. That's all.'

'Fascinating. I happen to know it was your gaunt associate Mr Edge who suffered that repellent complaint.' The doctor's laugh was harsh. 'You know what Bingo Violaine would have said about you, laddie? "The need to convince is unique to plain men." And if you were in the head, where was the brain?'

Gregor felt like a mime caught in the headlights. 'What?'

'Where's the brain?' Doctor Perfect demanded, leaning forward so that his skull tackle threatened to tip into Gregor's face like a jelly. 'There's two ways we can do this, laddie – the easy way, or the hard way. I've decided that we're going to do it the hard way. So just say whatever comes into your head.'

'What'll you do?'

'I'll do the same. This friend of yours – Barny. You seem to idolise him.'

'Not really. He eats trolls, after all. When he's nervous.'

'Trolls are just mimic vegetation. At the purely physical level they're a sort of wild fungus.'

'Well *he* doesn't think it's such wild fun. And my name's not Gus.'

'Perhaps. Tell me in your own words, what's the look of an elephant?'

'An ant.'

'The same?'

'Bigger and deformed.'

'Same noise?'

'Magnified.'

'To the power of?'

'A million.'

'What do you see in this inkblot?'

'A brain.'

'And this?'

'A brain.'

'And this?'

'A brain.'

'And this?'

'A brain.'

'And this?'

'A brain.'

'And this? A brain I'll bet, eh laddie?'

'Yes, yes a brain, how can I think of anything else with that suppurating lump of slime sat on your head like a rotting frog!'

'*What?*'

'Your *brain*, doctor, your *brain* – let me outta here!' Gregor sat up and shoved at his inquisitor. Stumbling backward, the doctor began shrieking incoherently – his brain had toppled from his head and hung between his shoulderblades, connected by a few taut arteries. He whirled around the dungeon, grasping backward like a harpy trying to zip herself up. The screams were outraged, wounded, inhuman. Gregor ran as fast as his arms and legs could take him.

Doomed Eddie Gallo sat smiling, the room a sunless forest of drying underwear. He looked up vaguely. 'Mr Edgy. How are you?'

'Enjoyment keeps me huge, doomed Eddie Gallo, you know me.'

'Yes I do. Siddown. I met that girl of yours – Amy. She was out there snogging a flower. I asked her its name and she said she didn't know. You young people today, eh?'

Edgy chuckled affably, admiring the room's adornments. 'You sure are the last word in underwear, doomed Eddie Gallo.'

'Think so?' The candidate radiated a shy pride.

'But be careful. Public biological steaming is considered a weakness in politics. The Mayor does his laundry behind bronze doors three foot thick. That's sort of what I need to chat about.'

'Lard cake?'

'No, thank you. So listen, what's with you and Barny?'

'Barny. Oh, he's great – a star.'

'You like him, right? So why put up thousands of posters all over town saying he's a bastard?'

'Oh, that was old Mr Hammer, some chap who wandered in here. Said he had a fishy master of some kind who'd back the whole nine yards, make me a present of it. Sure you won't have some lard?'

'What did Hammer look like?'

'Tall. Heavy coat. Clearly a stranger to the climate round here. Had a big, stretched nose. No eyes at all. Below that, jowls. Took only five hundred biscuits in return. It's all right, Barny agrees to the whole thing.'

'Where'd you get that pretty idea?'

'Hammer said so.'

'D'you believe everything you're told, doomed Eddie Gallo?'

'Why not? What did that Villain say? "An original hides his confusion." '

'Violaine. And it's "Confusion hides its origins". This campaign of yours has got Barny canned from the sorting office and pounced on by one and all. An old woman punched the front of his face near Snorter's. You've got to change your policy.'

'I don't mind. I'd no intention of causing distress. As a matter of fact I'm not sorry to change. I'd prefer something sunnier anyway. I saw a dog the other day – something about dogs, perhaps?'

'Dogs are good for nearly anything.'

'Think so? Whatever it is, it'll need to involve some sort of row or disagreement. That's how it works, apparently.'

'Dogs stare. Pant. Fight in the street.'

'Really?'

'It means nothing to them. I'm writing a book about it. It'll make my fortune, why not?'

'A book, with pictures? What's it called?'

'I think there'll be one picture, an oil painting. But they keep re-thinking the title. They've changed it now to *Savaged Beyond Repair*.'

'I'll look out for that.'

'You've got my vote, doomed Eddie Gallo.'

Mayor Rudloe welcomed a young *Blank Stare* reporter into his office. 'Sorry to bring you all the way up here – I'm up to my proud face in vital paperwork as you can see. And here you are, full of bones and spirit. Well done.'

'Thank you, Mr Mayor.' The journalist sat and flipped open a notebook.

'Well, you can be proud, coming out into the field –

journalists are the butter in society's backside – pardon the terminology but I'm another one who likes to tell it like it is, you and me alike. I wish I was in a real position of power, such as yourself – I'm just a servant of the people, what do I know? I'm just a man. Cures are still hostage to nature, as our great philosopher said. I'm at your disposal.'

The journalist related unconfirmed reports that a group of protesters had stood outside Barny Juno's house, wringing their hands so hard they wore down like soap. 'Apparently they all left with tiny hands.'

'This sort of thing doesn't surprise me in the least. The man known as Barny Juno is walking streets for which he is manifestly unqualified. He's unpalatable, devious, given to fits of rage, his manner wild and truculent and, yes, he's quite the waste of time. You might say he's the mutant in society's boiler room.'

'Have you met Juno?'

Rudloe laughed without a shred of meaning. 'I have reports that he gads about with an actual zombie. It wears sparring gloves, if you can believe it.'

'Do you believe it?'

'I believe whatever is necessary for the continued well-being of this community. Another of his friends is a man with a transparent head, filled with cloudy water. Now I ask you, is that any way to run a set of blameless associations. It seems that if anything stays still long enough, he'll befriend it. The man's drunk on his own power. Thriving like a bastard while the sun sets on us all.'

'Why don't you send in the militia before he wigs out completely? Do you have some serious reservations?'

The Mayor leaned back and demonstrated that he could puff his cheeks out with the best of them. 'That's a large subject. There is no precedent for such an action. Meaning, we've never set the militia upon this particular man before. But they are maintaining a state of constant readiness and I've made it perfectly clear that I will not hesitate to devise a sacramental penalty to the satisfaction of jeer and justice, subject to procedure. This knife will not forever sleep in my head. And it is my considered opinion that, for whatever fantastic reason, Juno is spoiling for censure. I offer no apology for my hard line on this matter. This community has a great many strengths and I will not see it dishonoured.'

'What do you see as those strengths?'

'I'm glad you asked. Two words. Two life-changing little words, my friend. Frisky skylarking. When I stand on my balcony and gaze down I see a people who are spirited, folksy and with no elite.' The Mayor set his jaw like the sternest of statesmen. 'I find it sad that one bad apple chooses to stretch and dye his earlobes for the sole purpose of instilling sick apprehension in the onlooker. And I make no bones about it – insolence and ostentation, biting at random, all the really back-breaking work of social outrage, these spell disaster for our community. And that's just a baffling fragment of my policy in that area.'

The reporter wound up with the usual question regarding rumours of an infestation of floor lobsters in the mayoral palace.

'Well now how could that be? Floor lobsters are the result of a corrupt environment.' The Mayor made a heavy stamping motion under the desk, smashing a scuttling carapace and covering the sound with a blustering cough. He shook hands again with the journalist while guiding him to the door.

When the journalist had left, Mayor Rudloe sank back into his own face. 'That'll put fish in his custard.'

'I ate all the headstones you brought,' Sweeney gurgled, the glass mask of his chestplate filling with bile. 'None of which will be of much use again.' The convolute emperor of white shell and gizzard shifted in his arterial chair. 'Worked wonders on the digestive tract.' He spread his ribs like a flashcoat, revealing intestines and a mothball heart.

Dietrich raised his black ice skull from the padlock embryos he'd been puzzling over. 'Frustration's fathom gold to us. Are you sure you want to go up there? You'll have to downsize a little.'

'The man's almost incoherently mellow. Harrowingly

honest. I'll unravel the conundrum of his guts.' Sweeney's own guts were pullulating, umbilical colours shining like china and framed by buck ribs which closed again like the jaws of a shark. As he sealed and hardened over, Sweeney's yellow eyes were distant, focused on inner processes.

'You're sure he's your enemy?'

'Does a stream flow on the seabed?' Sweeney replied, and clouted Dietrich's nose with a vague gesture. He pushed down on the arms of the shell throne, his hydraulic gullet dumping black ink in a damburst. 'Well, it's iffy, you're right. But the wheels of hell turn slow. Shift gears occasionally.' At the join, spinal resin stretched, snapping, leaving rounds of shell like a king prawn hull. Sweeney straightened up, dangling semi-liquid and gushing bloodwater. 'Vast future, I squash you in the nursery.'

Sliding his shadow along, so thick it was almost a voice, he became a silhouette before blue alcohol flames.

He squinted to perceive a horizon churning with targets. Though too small for even a demon's eyes, I withdrew through miles of rock into utter safety.

10

House Tornado

All life wears a surface for your glance,
like you're doing now

Barny had a brief natter with Feral Beryl, a useless old hag who lived in the swamp, knew nothing of interest and wanted to be left alone. The notion that she was wise persisted through the gobsmacked embarrassment of her inquisitors and their subsequent falsification of the wisdom received. No one liked to admit they'd just been screamed at and kicked savagely in the balls.

When Barny arrived at his parents' shack he was still gasping from the Beryl attack and, leaning into the moth cage to kiss Ramone hello, sucked the silvery creature into his mouth.

'You brought a paper?' Ma Juno barked from her concrete chair.

Barny swallowed reflexively. 'Er . . . no mother.' He slammed the moth cage and became brisk. 'I see the hair's still attached and thriving, father. Let's go on to the porch and check it out.'

'What?' Pa Juno was bewildered as Barny hauled him by the arm.

'Go, Henry,' cackled Ma Juno. 'He's your son, not mine.'

Swamp glue crawled past the porch. The darkness zipped with springloaded gobs and blurring stings.

Pa Juno's plasmate hair was palpitating slowly, aglow like a fluorescent kraken. He spoke in a low, confidential tone. 'I think I understand why you wanted to get out of there.'

'Oh?' Barny choked.

'Saw the paper. BARNY JUNO RELEASES CROC IN PACKED THEATRE. Hid it from your mother, on the floor of the moth cage. Another headline like that'd break her heart. I'd like to know what exactly you hoped to achieve when you did a thing like that.'

'I've got a problem with the Horned One, father.'

'Why you coughing, you got a cold? You on drugs?'

'Something in my throat. So what do you think I should do?'

'If she's that horny, stick with her. You think *you* know fear?' Pa Juno glanced cautiously in through the stained window. 'That woman married me to within an inch of my life. A vacuum kills guarantees, boy. A maggot turns into a butterfly, a lover turns into a maggot.'

Barny had already heard about his parents' early relationship. At the wedding they exchanged rings with such venom the priest let out a small cry.

'And you damn well better mark my words because I know this – it's like cooking someone from frozen, it takes a while. That's how it is when you know the complicated pain of marriage . . .'

Stunned with boredom, Barny watched the light and shadow cast on torn wood by his father's undulating locks.

'Remember what I always told you?'

'Er . . . never eat grapes.'

'Not that, boy.'

'Hold the hen and I'll do the rest.'

'No.'

'Broken glass at street corners is vitamin C.'

'No, I told you happiness functions best in bed. So hang on to Magenta Blaze. Know what I pray of a morning? That god should leave me alone if he can. That, Joe, is my brief opinion.'

'Well my name's not Joe, but I see what you mean.'

Ma Juno exploded from the house shrieking, 'Gone –

Ramone is gone, oh my papery boy' or something like that and Barny knew the jig was up. 'Look what your son put in his place.' She held up the newspaper with the croc headline and her face roared off in all directions.

'I never released a croc – and anyway it was an alligator. Its legs are delicate.'

'Oh they're delicate are they,' sobbed his mother. Pa Juno held her, scowling at Barny. 'Flimsy. Well what about the thin, silvery wings of Ramone? My tiny quivering fluff-faced child. He was more of a son than you'll ever be.'

'And you're no son of mine,' said Pa Juno.

The shaman Beltane Carom glanced at the poster of the jet black demon, its filed teeth and fungal white eyes. 'I know of a fiend designed along those lines. Articulated. Bayonet ears. Sweeney.'

Edgy was stood in Carom's yard, a tile court worked into neat geometries. The walled sanctuary was scattered with barnacle leaves. 'What would it want with Bubba? It's levering the election – you seen the paper here?' Edgy slapped the *Blank Stare*. 'Drunk with power, says the Mayor. Barny's never been drunk with anything.'

Carom was a mild, soft-spoken man, not given to drama. He gave the thing proper consideration. 'Sweeney sits at the hub of a billion creepchannels – a lot on his plate. Maybe Juno's got something this demon wants. Or Juno took something from him. You know when you take the heart, or the spine? Or whatever of a demon? The motorcord fluid's a fine natural weedkiller.'

'Natural?'

'Well maybe not. There's a defector demon living here in Accomplice but I don't think he's involved. Juno's into animals, right?'

'The winged and stepping animals of the earth, right, he lives for them.'

'Maybe Sweeney covets one of those. He's a soul eater. Marinates them delicately in the creepchannel nets. Considers modern souls are too bland without it.'

'Barny's not a channel racer. Hasn't got the hardware, them fancy motors with the nerve chassis. Doesn't interest him.'

'Folk wander in by accident. Most people suspect the existence of these adjacent realms as one nostril suspects the existence of the other.' Carom gazed at a little sun balancing on a leaf, though there was no sun in the sky. 'Or maybe something about Barny sticks in the demon's craw zone or gullet area.'

'I don't get it.'

'When a monster passes, we take it for another whose favourable opinion we must seek. Barny doesn't because he's unaware of that stuff. Not dumb, just totally preoccupied.'

'I know what you mean. I saw him carrying a church bell made of jelly one time. He dropped it and started crying. Eight squirrels and eleven birds came down out of the trees and sat on his shoulders. It looked like they were whispering comfort into his ears.'

'I wouldn't like to have nineteen animals on *my* shoulders.' Carom absently shuffled a stack of meat cards as big as a loaf of bread. 'I was there when Mister Spiderman's funeral blew up in Barny's face. Mayhem of a very particular type does seem to accrete around the guy.'

'Okay well I'm meeting the gang up the Anti, wanna come?'

Carom begged off, saying he had to explore his dark side.

'I'm supposed to do something for the Plunder Parade,' said B.B. Henrietta, smoking a cigar. Most of the crew were in the Anti Room, a club accidentally bonegrown from a drifting spore. The walls were rippled and ribbed, slimy white, sporadically flushing and pumping with fluorescent smears. Sometimes cinderblocks were lowered quickly from the ceiling on tarry rope, injuring or otherwise inconveniencing the revellers before being drawn up again.

'So?' asked Edgy.

'I don't wanna.'

'What about the amateur dramatics et cetera? That production you did of *I Love Strutting* a few months ago was a riot. People were screaming with laughter. I pissed myself.'

'Edgy, people were screaming *because* you pissed yourself. That's what caused the riot. Even you weren't laughing. I just don't feel like standing on a float dressed as a cake or whatever, I'd rather watch.'

'Amy'll be disappointed, I think she's writing something.'

'Oh god. What?'

'A recital or something. I think it's about eyelids.'

'Eyelids.'

'So? Yes, eyelids. Anything wrong with that? Give her some support.'

'She's your girlfriend, Edgy, it's your place to support her goddamn eyelids.'

'But the Parade's traditional.'

'So's death and decay.'

Fang, cutting a sorry figure in stripes of duct tape, was staring at oblivion in a corner and didn't comment.

'I'll watch,' B.B. continued. 'From the Tower.'

'The guard guy Murdster won't let anyone up there. Some kinda trouble with the moral fibre a few years back.'

'I know all about it.'

'You don't know.'

'Oh I know the story.'

'On the fibre?'

'Oh yeah.'

'So?'

'Made of ham.'

'No.'

'And a dog got it.'

'Dogs don't eat ham.'

'They sure as hell don't eat moral fibre, Scarecrow. You see ads for dogfood saying "with added moral fibre"?'

Gregor came back from the bathroom and sat down. 'So I went to the shrink. Left him shrieking, with his entire brain hanging right down on some nerves. Says I should go pamper my statue. You know what? I might even do it.'

'Really?'

'I can take or leave it. I suppose I'm just clutching at straws.'

'Well keep that to a minimum, Round One. Remember the crop circle disaster.'

A year earlier a massive crop circle had appeared in the exact likeness of Gregor's face.

'Where's Barny?'

'Gone to see Feral Beryl. I guess if anyone knows what's going on, it's her.' Edge downed his drink. 'That Bubba, he's got a head on him like a baby dog.'

B.B. Henrietta frowned. 'You mean a puppy?'

'A head like a puppy, that's right.'

Fang perked up. 'Who's got a head like a puppy?'

'Bubba,' Edgy told him. 'And it's getting younger and glossier by the minute.'

'That's not what it says in the *Stare*. According to that he's drunk with power.'

'According to the Mayor,' grunted Edgy with disgust. 'Enough of the yammer. I'm dancing.'

'You're going to dance?' said Gregor. 'Why don't you just stab us in the heart.'

B.B. honked with laughter.

Edgy got up, walking off as music began flushing the capillaries in the wall. Edgy had created a dance called 'The Last Straw'. Mankind, plodding and perishable, would never be equal to this flailing freak-out. Passing fungal tables and rib-caged lightbulbs, alternately staggering under some killing weight and sloshing back and forth in an exhausted way, he reached the dancefloor and began a set of murky and obscure manoeuvres. He seemed at first to be climbing against a landslide. Soon he was arc-welding a large copper melon. Then he pumped one arm as though mashing the face of a monk against a rippled glass partition. Now he was trying to stuff an octopus into an overhead luggage rack. Next came something like a frantic yank at an emergency cord – the invisible cord came away in his hand, wrapping round him like a snake. Or perhaps he was chasing his coat arm like a dog after its tail. Then he began windmilling his arms in shockingly arbitrary vortices, volleying barely audible shouts above the music. Finally his body detonated into a trashing mazurka, the tantrum of a lifetime, a dance which, appended to his human qualities, rendered him temporarily into a more perilous species.

Like snowflakes, no two fistfights are the same. When a strange raver approached Edgy – one togged up like some giant white mantis, all slick and fluted – Edgy was pitching a fit which seemed the hairtrigger release of a lifetime's rage. Amid strobe-glimpses of zombies having a tough time, hectic bone dust and benthic wall channels, the stranger's pelt of sickly yellow leather was glistening open to show a black latticework of nerve barbs. Tormented by loose-jointed convulsions and releasing sporadic yelps, Edgy whirled loose, kicking him with an arm that wasn't good for much else. A set of mantrap teeth spun into the shadows.

Opening his eyes a short time later, Edgy was becoming dimly aware that he had struck someone – but his attention was caught by Neville Peth and his wife, who was as primly pretty as a paper doily. They were sat in a booth and seemed out of place here, evidently slumming. But Edgy's performance had them agape. What a godsend!

'That guy shouldn't have got in my way!' Edgy shouted, spotlit and tussling with his own stomach. 'I'm harebrained and reckless, I don't mind saying. A beacon for trouble! I could even join a club for hazardous activities!' He stanced wide, beckoning the masses. 'Come on! Come on, I'll take you all on! I don't care what danger I'm inviting!'

Disgusted, Neville Peth and his wife shuffled out of the booth and skittered away toward the exit.

'I love the glories of danger!' Edgy called after them as they slammed out. He looked back to find himself surrounded by growling adversaries.

Ropes of gore hanging from his broken mouth, Sweeney flung himself down a side alley. In one wall was a mundane door over which he had superimposed a gore gate. He stepped into this now and was folded down to a pain bandwidth where he hung in the chiming cold. Dietrich floated up to him, bile corpuscles bouncing off his breastplate. 'I told you, he's a nutter.'

11

Musette

A single punch can be directed toward a waiter and your own advantage

Barny was fortunate in having a couple of back-up father figures. The first was Mr Peterson, who sat forever poolside with a drink the same colour as his tan. Peterson owned a few hydro farms and basked in this and other facts. He had a fat, friendly smile and a right hand made of coloured glass. Barny drove a car for him once when a friend of Mr Peterson had to run from a noisy building. Mr Peterson appreciated this kindness so much that he listened to Barny's problems now and again, though whatever the problem was, Mr Peterson put it down to women. Barny found a broken cabbage near a rusty generator one time and Mr Peterson said the problem was with women.

'This your idea of a dark night of the soul, Barny?' Mr Peterson asked now. 'A few housecalls? Tea?'

'Got any biscuits?'

'Drink this – it'll put hair on your grave. So what's happening in the random world?'

'I seem to be having some kind of problem with the devil, Mr Peterson.'

'No, Barny. Your only problem is with women. It's like you to blame it all on some vengeful mutant. Eh? What are we dealing with here? Fuzzy thinking, Barny, you being the worst offender. I mean here you are, a young guy, with okay looks and a cock as big as all outdoors. You could have any girl you wanted. And you got the real, dyed-in-the-wool, water-on-the-snaredrum unoriginality to hang around with someone like the Blaze, just for the looks of her. Insulting to her too, if you want the raw truth of it. And I know how it is, there's certain images make an ache in a sensitive man. Like Bardot hugging that baby seal. Wouldn't you like to just jump in there? So what if she was blond? So was Bardot and it served her well.' Mr Peterson gestured across the pool to the allotment, where Mrs Peterson was crouching amid transparent, pullulating globes. 'She's in my blood and my understanding. I don't know any more what she looks like to other people. I'd want that for you, Bubba.'

'Is your wife growing jellyfish, Mr Peterson?'

'Never you mind. I don't wanna get into the whole thing with you here, but go with a girl where you have to be faking it and you'll strip your gears. An honest relationship's as satisfying as drawing in Biro on a banana.'

'Good then?'

'That's what I'm telling you. God almighty, Bubba. I'm saying faking doesn't take, except as a terrible sickness. I remember one time, a beautiful girl asked me if I could ride a horse. I said I could, of course I could ride a horse. In fact I was racking my brains to remember what a horse was. She wanted to take me riding.'

'Did you fall off the horse, Mr Peterson?'

'No, I was fine actually. Damnedest thing. I thought I'd fold like a cloth hat.'

Barny looked at the slow surface of the water.

'So, er, what shall I do about this devil problem, Mr Peterson?'

'Ah there you go Bubba, getting all agitated. All right, here it is, something I read once, I always remembered it. From me to you. "Age is not care, starvation is not understatement, thoughts are not invocations." Eh? What, too rich for your blood? Just talking to you's exhausting, you know that? God almighty. Okay, get this simple set-up into your skull, Bubba. Men love women. Women can't handle how much men love them. Men get confused. There you have it. Now leave me alone, I'm eating a sandwich here.'

The other paternal fallback ran the Juice Museum, a repository of ignored stories, rejected wisdom and forgotten capers based in a derelict stone watchtower near the sea. It was in the nature of the Juice Museum that it went almost totally unacknowledged by the populace.

Mr Low, an old man with a face as furry as a dust ventilator, was stocktaking when Barny arrived. If Barny was after tea he'd come to the right place – Low drank more than was required to kill him, and hallucinated. His tea genie appeared to him in the deeps of evening, chattering about sand slues and starched delicate bombers, shredded linen draping through them like ghosts. Barny made deliberate noise as he entered the small storeroom. It was a place of instrument chairs, escaped filigree, police trees and clock lanterns – plenty of stuff to clatter.

'Eh? Juniper my boy, I'm sorting a bunch of Maraffi sketches. Anything else of the sort. Map of the demi-maze.' Low pointed to an involuted diagram which trailed into vague waves at one end. 'Tally sticks,' he said, picking up and discarding some notched wood. 'Heart dust in a smoked bottle, seashells gone to sleep in offices, glass eyes chipped in a playground, a dead baby as the result of language, the sound of an illusion ageing, a dozen tumour gods, and this box here. Wood is time tided.' He opened the small wooden box and his face glowed with the fluttering light. 'The resin-scented dark of a fir forest, eyelash afternoons of flybuzz, trams smelling of thunderstorms.' He shut the box and tossed it aside.

'I need your advice Mr Low.'

Low sat on a chair as fragile as himself, breathing hard. 'Ah. Your problem with the Mayor and so on, I saw the paper, you're drunk with power now, it seems.' He trotted his tongue on the roof of his mouth. 'You're a decision grafted on to confusion, Juniper. No solution. Ill-matched, oil and water. But you'll serve, you see? It's an old trick but folk forget so as to be fooled over and entertained. Denial on all fronts. Weather wasn't always like this, you know that? This heat. Tropical storms. People forget it rained painfully cold back a way. Started with the loss of nature. Love concrete and the moon's dirt, you see? Measurement razors the sky, wintering history. New songs eat at the nets and stone lips pocket the truth. Look at this.'

Low reached into a tea crate and dragged out a plate of hammered tin. 'Kelman's Deadly Sombrero – hazardous titanium headgear worn by Jack Kelman, a stoker long deceased. Here's an otherwise unremarkable man, never sought liberty, dated no stars, went away unknown – but left this in testament.' He rummaged again, bringing out more arcane salvage. 'Flower's Joyce Belt. A True Polychrome Lad. The Barefaced Cheek. The Skeleton of Manila's Moustache.'

'Who's Manila?'

'I don't entirely know. And these sea-stained books here exist despite the entrenched scepticism of the official line – *Cable's Diary*. Got a book on the Glass Alphabet with pictograms and all. Learnt some.' He chirped strangely. '*Doll Apocrypha*. And here are the *Violaine Prophecies*.'

'Violaine's not forgotten, Mr Low – he's a what-do-you-call-it, a brainsaver. When people go a long time without thinking.'

'But few people know about the *Prophecies*. He said this stuff while a demon was eating his brain. Listen to this: "Where the word goes, evil follows." Not up to his usual standard is it? And what have we got here, the *Silvane Letters*.'

'The *Silvane* what?'

A dark-haired girl appeared in the doorway. 'The Wesley Kern Gun, father.' She was holding something which looked like a twist of bleached beachwood.

'You've met Chloe, Juniper.' Mr Low stood to take the relic. 'This belongs downstairs,' he said, and shuffled out. The girl came over and sat on a table, looking at Barny with eyes as black as concord grapes.

Barny had last glimpsed her against the bitter bile-light of the creepchannel. He wasn't sure he'd ever seen her here. Barny was again completely hypnotised by her bare white feet. He wanted to kneel and lick upward until his face was buried in her fur. 'What's your favourite accident?' she asked suddenly.

'Uh? Oh . . . flying bar of iron.'

'End to end?'

'Yes, from a building site to a passer-by.'

'Me too.' She looked at him like a beady-eyed wombat. 'Are you all right? Worried about the animals?'

Barny was watching how each sentence strummed the sinews of her throat. 'Golden Sid's at the house,' he said absently.

'Golden Sid?'

'Yeah. Yeah, he's a class act. And I've put dark glasses on the 'gator.' He told her about the mob which had been picketing his house until the lion, chased by hunger, exploded through a window and galloped down the gangplank, feasting someone to the ground. 'As luck would have it it was just a tailor.'

She looked as if she cut her own hair. Barny thought the dreams underneath would be the warmest and safest in the world – that's how bad it had gotten already. She was talking about something and swinging her legs back and forth. Somehow because she was barefoot she was completely naked to him there on the table. 'Like the little triggers inside an insect,' she was saying. Her mouth was so big it cut her head in half.

'Uh?'

'Wesley Kern.'

Barny stood up like a robot. 'Well, it's been good, but I've got to go and help Sid now with the leopard, who's a bit moody since I had a meat gargoyle clinging to the roof over there. I hope to see you again.'

Walking out with the awkwardness of a rod-puppet, he felt like a man leaving a bank with a gold bar in his pants.

Becoming a little desperate, Barny went to consult the

Church of Automata re his problems. He didn't know much about doll worship and had it pictured as a listening head on larynx, tilting a little with each statement, shit-scary. He rapped at a door made of solid diamond and, seeing it nudge open, began to relate his tale. But the head poking from the doorcrack was a worn china skull inset with smoked glass eyes. Barny started screaming, a Doll Engineer swept out and, instantly apprised of the situation, tore the belt from Barny's pants for the purpose of thrashing the living daylights out of him.

Hammering at the door of the Powderhouse a short time later, Barny was greeted by a Fusehead with party streamers hanging from his ears. Beltless, Barny's pants descended. The affronted priest slammed the door in his face and opened it again to beam at the damage.

A while later Barny was sifting for scraps in a trashcan out back of the chef school. He needed meat for the animals but all he could find was pasta. Noises from inside – the back door was ajar – Barny peered through.

The instructor Quandia Lucent, who also ran the Ultimatum Restaurant, was strutting up and down before the initiates. 'Perfection including tip,' he was saying. 'Behold.'

And he opened the double doors of a garishly painted cabinet. Inside hung a seahorse the size of a child, its ragged gills quivering like lettuce. The initiates gasped, kneeling. 'There is detestable dinner made,' said the seahorse in an eerie, quailing voice, 'eventually someone must retrieve it. Thus, we thrive.'

'We thrive,' the initiates repeated.

'Try explaining tyranny,' the seahorse sibilated, 'without using the word "pasta". These fools can't get enough of it. If a genie gave them three wishes, they would select pasta for all three.'

'Recite the creed,' snapped Quandia Lucent.

'Garbage,' called the initiates. 'At crippling prices.'

The gang were at Snorters cafe. Edgy had not remained unaffected by his encounter with the eight-foot mantis, and was telling Barny about it. Only one of his legs had been broken in the later brawl and he felt like a lucky man. 'Punched something, apparently. Rhymes with "demon".'

'Was it a demon?'

'Yes. Purporting to be a normal fella.'

'That dance of yours is a heck of a deal.'

'It wasn't purporting to be normal,' stated B.B. Henrietta for the record. 'It was like the thing in the posters, but white.'

'But you know what it's all about now, right Bubba? Feral Beryl explained it all.'

'No,' said Barny. 'She just screamed at me and kicked me savagely in the balls.'

'Well you must have done something to offend her.'

'Then I swallowed Ramone. My mother thinks I stole him and set him loose on the community.'

'That's tough, Bubba,' said Edgy. 'How about you replace it with a cigarette butt.'

'I think they'll notice the difference,' B.B. Henrietta pointed out as though speaking to a child. 'You do know there's a difference, right?'

'Well not everyone has my razor-sharp perceptions, baby. I have to be that way, the life I live in the Motel. In fact the sensations in my extremities are seven times more intense than those of the average man. With their richness and distinction, I could sell my leg perceptions alone for a mint.'

'Extra strong?'

'That's what I've been telling you.'

Gregor chipped in, stirring his coffee. 'Maybe Bubba should say he tracked the moth down, then buy another one, show it to 'em.'

Edgy intercepted this. 'No, they'll know right away – you think moths are uniform, featureless, then look at one close up and it's got the face of Walter Matthau.'

'You wish,' snorted B.B. Henrietta.

'So what are you doing for the Parade finally, little missy? What do I tell Ms Gort?'

'Tell her what you like, I'm not doing it.'

'Okay, just play merry hell with everything. Things being how they are, she'll have to do a reading. And god help us all.'

'What's so bad about the poetry?' asked Barny.

'She's got theories, Bubba. Says it should come naturally. It should blend with nature. So when people hear her read it they should respond like nothing's happened.'

'So what is it, pastoral stuff? Flowers?'

'No, it's terrible. I don't understand what the hell's going on. She's got this thing called "I Freeze and Smash the Velvet". I hear it, I feel like I'm reversing down a skyride. She's wanting me to get her published by Feeble Champ Books, like I've got any influence.'

'So how's the dog book going?' asked Gregor.

'Really well, Round One. I've done a few more chapters: Casino Dogs, Dogs in a Warm Breeze, Dogs Who Change Directions, Dogs Who Sin Against Me, Dogs With Blurred Legs, Tramlike Dogs Who Shuffle, er . . . Dogs With Weepy Eyes, Tapdancing Dogs, Dogs Who Know But Don't Say, Dogs Who Enlist, Dogs With More Than Five Ears, Dogs Who Freeze Solid and er . . . oh yeah, Labradors. But Feeble Champ went and changed the title again.'

'To what.'

'*When Dogs Seize Control*. They don't know what the hell they're doing. And the marketing plan's conspicuous by its absence. So I've decided to kind of advertise it myself at the Parade. Me and some dogs, with a sign about the book. It'll go down a blast.'

'What about the cover,' Gregor said. 'The oil painting. You with your arm round the Dalmatian's shoulder.'

'Alsatian,' Edgy corrected. 'Anyway they seem to have forgotten about it. They want a photograph of a dog, now, walking along a path. It's insanity. But never mind all that.' Edgy adopted a wily, confidential tone. 'Because while everyone else has been out eating moths I've been consulting an authority on matters demonic about Barny's situation. Answer me this, Bubba. The 'gator, where did you find it?'

'In some slime in a creepchannel wall.'

'Well there you go, the worst I suspected. You're not a creep racer, that kind of commute takes nerves of steel, Bubba, steel.'

'Fang goes through sometimes.'

'Bubba, how can I ever make you understand – Fang's dead. He's a really old dead guy walking around. Why do you think he drinks embalming fluid? Sleeps in a peat bog? His head's black and swollen like a bowling ball.'

Barny chuckled to himself. 'He's great, isn't he?'

'Yes he is.'

'He's a tough hombre.'

'But listen Bubba, this creep entrance, where was it?'

'Well you know how it is, you never know where they are until you're near and you remember, so there it is suddenly, and afterwards you don't remember again.'

'Because it's semi-etheric, right? Like how you forget a dream. But you know the general area?'

'I remember I was walking Help in the Furfur district, around the scrub near the skeleton coast road.'

'Case closed. That reptile's been doped with knowhow from the creepchannel,' Edgy concluded. 'Maybe it's even smart and that's why it hasn't bitten the hell out of you. The demon wants his bone back. Say it with me, people.'

'I've never understood the Announcement Horse,' muttered Gregor vaguely, gazing into space. 'What's he meant to be, a robot? Another statue, made of metal? Does he eat hay like a normal horse? What's the deal, has anyone ever asked him?'

'Doctor Perfect says it's just armour filled with heavy smoke,' said B.B. Henrietta.

'Has anyone heard a thing I've said?' barked Edgy.

'I was behind the chef school,' Barny began to confide haltingly. 'Earlier on. And I overheard the chefs talking, taking orders from – from a giant seahorse in a painted cabinet. Talking all about pasta. Oh Edgy it scared me.'

'Of course it's scary, it's inescapable.'

Edgy stopped, gasping.

'Pasta. That's it.'

He clattered his bone crutches into place, and tilted out of the cafe.

12

The Scar Garden

A man without error is a geographical impossibility

Barny showed up at the mayoral palace and was taken to Rudloe's office. Max Gaffer's eyeball abacus bust and went everywhere. 'Very foolhardy, Juno,' said the Mayor, standing. 'You come in here tracking mud all over my campaign. Oh, you don't need to tell me. You want I should hold off, go easy on you. I need hardly remind each of you that 'gator's teeth is a snag in my plans.' The Mayor turned to Max Gaffer. 'Eh?'

'Outstanding, sir.'

The Mayor was getting into the stride. 'Carnivore on a short fuse? I don't think so. Thrashing? Not in this town. We deal with the Steinway Spiders don't we? I intend to spearhead speculation as to your irrefutable guilt in this matter.'

Barny sat down amiably. 'Hey you look like a Weeble toy,' he blurted in delighted surprise. 'I've been trying to work it out.'

Uncertain, the Mayor seated himself also. 'All right, I've heard enough. You know, in my darker moments I rue the fates for making me mayor of a place so obscure it's where ants go to die. People frying eggs on their cars *all* goddamn day. I feel exhausted just talking about it. This position involves more than just pointing a crusher at some tame flunky, you know. Which reminds me.' He picked up the phone. 'Erno – get these clattering vermin squared away will you?'

Erno came in with a metal hook and started swiping at the floor, and Barny realised there were three huge corruption bugs on the carpet. Not for the first time, Barny wondered whether these creatures were related in any way to the thing that had birthed from Dumbar's head. The number of legs differed, alas.

'You see, Juno, it's like this. You can't go wrong spending money on death and murder. A lot of people have noticed it through the years. But besides the appalling expense, why squander the goodwill of the electorate immediately? All we need is deceit, an enemy, and negligence. Phrase horrors like an invitation and you'll get a crowd. Ask Sidebar Billy over there. Even the pessimist believes he'll finally acquire others' respect amid rubble. Of course by that time I'll be dead and swelling the strawberries. Eh Max?'

'Outstanding, sir.'

'So crawling in here trying to bargain, Juno, you're walking on dangerous water. Between you and me the Conglomerate have got it all tied up anyway. You're mining your own road. Give it up.'

'I'm not sure what you mean by all that, Mr Mayor, but I'm pleased to meet you.'

'So what do you want?'

'I'm looking for a job.'

'A job?'

'Yeah, as a doorman, a bodyguard, anything you like.'

'A job.'

'Beggars can't be choosers, ma'am.'

'I don't believe it,' the Mayor groped. 'I don't . . . tell me why the hell I should give you any kind of a job here.'

'I think shoes should be sold in big jars. Like gherkins.'

The Mayor leaned forward, enunciating carefully. 'Do you understand that I'm basing my campaign on a demonisation of you and your supposed depravities?'

'Eh?'

'I don't believe it, you're a fantastic moron. Hey, what's with the troll? Oh my god.'

'Mmmmffshff.'

'Oh, mother of mercy. Max, are you seeing this?'

'Outstanding, sir.'

'In my whole life I've never . . .' The Mayor fell silent as, crossing some inner threshold, his rage boiled into focus. He swelled with malice. 'Get out. That's right: out.'

Barny stood calmly, smiled in bewilderment at all present, and left. As the door wafted shut behind him he heard the Mayor snarl something about waking the Brigade.

'Agree,' thought B.B. Henrietta, 'and he'll believe he's thinking.' She had a mop of blond hair like the seedhead of a dandelion and failed to inform the relevant authorities. She approached the Tower of Nowt and banged loud at the door.

Murdster the Sentinel opened up, glowering.

'You make that look so easy,' grinned B.B. Henrietta.

A beefy man with a boilerplate forehead, Murdster seemed always in a foul and vengeful mood. When mixed with his surprise at B.B.'s temerity, this resulted in something resembling contemplation. 'I'm locked in my safety.'

'You certainly are.'

'Tradition doesn't play.'

'But that's so sad.' B.B. altered her head angle, tipping it carefully aside.

'Snort and people adjust their ears.'

'I know what you mean.' A slumping nod.

'Ears won't live for ever – anyway they're like erasers.'

B.B.'s giggling skills were badly marred by cigar use but she had a go.

'They call me stone face.'

'That's horrible and it's not true.'

'Sober yet all aflame, the new sinners time their generosity.'

'Oh I agree.'

'You want something from me.'

'Bargain Basement Henrietta. And I see there's no fooling you, Mr Murdster sir.'

*

It's difficult for a man made of a single muscle to look shifty – this was to the slab-bodied G.I. Bill's advantage. Still smarting from his recent defeat in the ballpark when Gregor had failed to show, he lurked after Barny and Gregor as they approached Scardummy Garden. The Garden was an ornate precinct containing statues of everyone in Accomplice – it was traditional to visit and decorate your statue with fancy clobber. Some never bothered, letting theirs overgrow with ivy. The statues changed over time and crumbled when the person died. A citizen could kill another by smashing the other's statue, but their own would shatter simultaneously, killing them by the karmic principle of statucide.

The weedy paths into this green-and-clean vista were fringed with radio discards, slash water, blown-out watches and jawflowers. Long logs lay shedding copper scales and red shreds. 'Let's deck the dummies and get out of here,' said Gregor wearily as they entered the huge standing landscape.

'I thought you were here on doctor's advice.'

'I don't know. He doesn't seem to have a good word to say for me. Maybe I can just tell him my dreams or something. They're the one thing about me that's definitely unbeatable. Last night I dreamt I picked off the shell of a waitress. Inside was a wallet.'

'And in the wallet?'

'Cannelloni.'

Colonnade gusts skittered leaves as Barny and Gregor strolled under a dome of dry plaster. Through the other side and pretty soon they were among statues, some plain and white, others dressed and made up, still others mottled and overgrown. The keglike statue of Gregor stood backed against a bush as though cornered by an advancing mob. It was half swallowed by a tide of weeds and lichen had cowled its head. Gregor started tearing feebly at the weeds, a look of distaste on his face.

G.I. Bill leaned behind a whiskered Stimson tree and listened to their blather.

'You make me nervous when you're quiet,' said Gregor.

'I think I'm going to hide out for a while. Edgy says the

'gator's valuable and unpopular. I think Mister Newton is a reptilian gentleman. The food rips as he shuts his gob.'

Gregor bitterly threw clumps of grass aside. 'Why do you keep telling me that – you think I don't know? It rips it rips, are you satisfied?'

'Golden Sid's a man among men. Behind those wire spectacles are his eyes and part of his head, that's for sure. But when it comes to getting him to speak in a normal voice, well, all you can say is he's a bastard to convince. You're going to have to help out in the evenings.'

Gregor straightened up. 'Eh? I'm not going in there with your goddamn monsters. I'll be reduced to a hundred treat bones for a dog. Remember what Violaine said? "Whether tears do good depends upon the philosophy of the onlooker." Those bastards won't hesitate for a second.'

'Why so tense, Round One? Don't you like animals at all?'

'I don't know, I mean, they don't speak. Why don't they speak? Are they proud? We're meant to guess?'

'They talk. Sometimes. I'm ready to listen. I'm ready, so should you be. Are you?'

'Am I ready to listen to animals talking, is that what you're asking me?'

'Yes.'

'Do I *look* like I'm ready?'

'But we're blessed by the winged and stepping animals of the earth. And cows. Don't you feel blessed by cows, Gregor?'

'*No* I don't feel blessed by cows. They stare at me. Like they're expecting something. Or like I've committed some crime and they know all about it. Plus when you walk through a field of cows, you don't know when one's going to decide to come up and indulge in some unwanted intimacy.'

'Are we talking about the same animal?'

'Yes a cow a cow, the big thing with the horns.'

'No, that's the devil, Gregor.'

Dumb but never idle, G.I. Bill slunk away with the greatest freight of knowledge his head would ever carry.

In fact Erno wasn't mute but nobody listened to him. He'd

said the Raj fan was a bad idea. Now he was up a ladder dismantling the thing. He decided the main support strut with the hidden microphone could stay for the moment. Below him the Mayor completed a phone call. 'The fee is agreed. Ten for the dog, eighty for this mysterious business with the gliding penguin.' As the Mayor slammed the receiver a thug barrelled into the room, Max Gaffer in pursuit.

'I got information about Juno!' shouted the guy.

'The spanner in the ointment,' said the Mayor, waving the lawyer back. 'What about him?'

'He's in the Scar Garden now! Says the 'gator's a gentleman! It's valuable! He's planning to disappear!'

'Now or never eh? You deserve as real a medal as we can manufacture from snot, whoever you are. God bless you sir, off you go.'

'Don't I get pay?'

'Let me be the judge of that. That's more than adequate from you.'

When G.I. Bill was gone, the Mayor stood. 'Shake my hand, Max. I'm a bastard.'

'All right, but don't touch the underwear.'

How can you recognise the sound of a sergeant and not learn the language of dogs? The dialects are almost identical. And the truth was, when the Sarge spoke the hounds came running.

The troops were stored in reverb space, a vault of repetition sealed from the thinking world. Shockwaves of smugness rocked out as the vault was unbolted. Within minutes of being thawed the Sarge was at a crusted mirror, shaving with an axe-head. Limbering up behind him was a crack team of utter bastards, pumped right up on unexamined rhetoric and ready for anything. Finished, he turned to his deputy, who brandished a dish.

'Snail, Sarge?'

'Don't mind if I do. What are they?'

'Snails, Sarge.'

'Snails. Don't mind if I do.'

'Get your face round that then.'
'What is it.'
'A snail, Sarge.'
'Snail. All right then. Eat it do I?'
'Eat it, Sarge, that's right.'
'What is it?'
'Snail – a snail, Sarge.'
'Snail.'
'A snail, Sarge. See? It's a snail.'
'Snail is it. Well now.'
'Snail.'
'Snail, eh. Well, don't mind if I do.'
'Good on yuh.'
'Right.'
'You eatin' it then?'
'Eh?'
'You eatin' that?'
'What is it.'

Before the deputy could reply, Max Gaffer came down with their orders and a look which said his underwear was forever beyond their reach.

Neville Peth looked up at a rapping sound and saw a ragged man on a cleaner's scaffold suspended outside the office window. The man, whose leg was in a cast, gestured frantically and seemed to be spooning pasta shells into his mouth. The man gave an exaggerated grimace, bucking as though sunk with venom.

Then the man seemed to be distracted, looking away. He quickly pulleyed the platform down and disappeared out of sight.

Neville Peth rose and went to the window, gazing down. A Brigade squad were stamping by below, followed by a ragtag pack of dogs. The thin man hobbled across the street to the gas station and stole a truck, peeling out and passing the troops. Neville Peth raised his eyebrows, found himself unequal to the effort and quickly lowered them again.

*

'Bubba, is that you?' Magenta Blaze appeared nearby. 'And the Worried One. Is that your statue? I always thought it was a boulder.'

'I've seen worse statues,' said Barny.

Magenta squinted at Gregor's statue as though at a bug. 'Than this?'

They went and watched Magenta decking her statue a while. She was plucking lashes from her vertebrae and slathering the face with stone makeup. 'So what you been up to, Bubba?' she asked, casual. 'Too preoccupied by your run-ins with the dark forces and being a social pariah to see your little Madge?'

Barny was transfixed with guilt.

'Couldn't even send me a letter?'

'A what?'

At that moment a truck exploded through a hedge, a busted statue on its hood. Edgy hung limp from the cab and gasped, 'I stole another truck from Mike Abblatia. Remember what Violaine said: "Don't expect sincerity from a man unless the tide's coming in." I think he meant that trust goes unnoticed until it's broken. Like so much else. Laws, nature, my leg.'

'What the hell are you talking about?' Gregor snapped.

'The troops are coming,' Edgy explained, and passed out.

Upon examination, the statue turned out to be G.I. Bill's. Its leg had smashed in the impact. At the same instant Edgy's leg, just beginning to set, had shattered again.

The Brigade arrived at Scardummy Garden and the Sarge ordered a containment. 'I don't want the perimeter penetrated – the joke is, drills unrestrained can do it easy.' He shouted through a trumpet. 'Surrender or we celebrate.'

The deputy rushed up. 'No one here, Sarge – just the statues.'

'Nature ramble due to lack of assailants,' the Sarge ordered. 'I want acorns, fallen bark and rotting stag beetles here in one quarter-hour. Go go go go.'

Soon a heap of detail lay in the clearing. The haul was

dappled, rich and varied. 'No sign of registration, Sarge. No serial numbers.'

'This one doesn't work, Sarge,' said a cadet, trying to push an acorn into his forehead.

'What are you doing, boy? What's this – a rotten inner tube, Perkins? Put it back.'

'Is this a groundnut, Sarge?'

'Yes it is, Ripper. They ripen underground and are used in confectionery and as a source for peanut oil. The presence of this alongside the acorns highlights the idiosyncratic mix of tropical and deciduous flora in the region. What you got there Gibbs, some moss?' A sudden caterwauling started up, growing louder. 'What the hell's that now?'

'It's them dogs again, Sarge. They're attracted by your voice.'

Twenty dogs bounded into the clearing, ripping through the nature pile in an explosion of twigs and leaves – the troops fell back in distress and disappointment. Perkins knelt sobbing and clutching a fern.

13

Living in Harmony

Don't unravel them – your ears are meant to be that way

Mr Low said of course Barny could stay in the Juice Museum a while, and welcomed the 'gator like a long lost brother. Chloe said nothing of the beard of drool Barny had been wearing when he last departed and busied herself settling the 'gator in. There was a massive dead lamp in the watchtower's belfry, as mysterious to Barny as the moral fibre. Mr Low took him up there to look out over the baffling ocean but said it was no place to hide. 'Not from the forces that are ranged against you,' said Low cheerfully. He led him down the main spiral staircase, descending lower than the levels Barny recognised. They were soon underground, walking sloped subterranean passages. 'A place like this needs shadows. For things to fall into – and crawl out of. Secrets soak up the abyss, some.' They passed caves of forgotten wings, pyramids of misinterpreted enterprise, boxes overflowing with fossil keys and the spent hair of beauties.

'Here,' said Low, stopping in a catacomb corner wedged with filing cabinets, 'are the biological archives.' He retrieved a stack of parchments and flicked through in a flash of anatomical shadows, an arm of nerves, a head of blades, wingspread diagrams pinned with annotation. 'Demons. They can appear as fast cracks driving through walls, plans and mourners. They'll have your shoulders cramped with meetings, reduce your thinking to the market, import conclusions. Or they can flaunt their biology. Some are living wounds. Some are solid beef. Some are raw and slack, unclassifiable. Some mere mechanisms. See these things like the underside of a crab? Disguise themselves as free tickets to a gig, then unfurl at night, scuttle in the mouth, bang. Some are almost transparent like pearls, and appear at the window. Some are havoc angels, some are slaves, some are infective defectors. Some will mischief your life into despair.' He continued to browse through the ancient papers, where sawtooth skulls and latticed ribs had been numbered and named by some cursed scholar. 'Skittermite,' said Mr Low, allowing Barny a mere glimpse of a deltoid head before turning the page. 'And your friend Sweeney – *demonid scarab gargantua*. Necrotic flesh laced with infernodyne veins. Craves human salt. A soul's like the average vitamin, Juniper – the body can't manufacture it.'

'So what do I do, Mr Low?'

'Well. Could have done a lot worse than have a silver-eyed demon rasp doom in your ear. And this fellow couldn't begin to fathom how its innards are laid out. Console yourself with that, eh?'

After a few days drinking human spine milk direct as through a straw, Sweeney replaced his jaw by visiting an etheric forge into which he tossed a priest, a timid triangle player and the priest's beloved Jag. A surge of rage drew the lava into needles, crusting the hole and cooling it into black metal. He ate a few bottom-dwelling phantoms and deemed it a sterling job.

Dietrich strode down the ramp, admiring a new bracelet made of a cat's ribcage. 'How's the gob, Your Majesty.'

Sweeney's mouth spat out a fireball. 'Bloating rotbodies tip in the surf and all's well. I found the greater part of our activity a lark and these new choppers'll paint the town red next time.'

'The Aspict's still having trouble getting anything on Juno. He's completely screened somehow. But I think there's someone I can talk to above.'

Sweeney was distracted, admiring his reflection in a mirror. 'Oh?'

'Someone familiar with the community. Tap his head and free the necessary.'

'All right,' Sweeney sighed. 'And if you see a car, wad oatmeal in the tailpipe. We might as well stupefy a few drivers.'

The mirror was full of chains.

G.I. Bill levered himself toward Barny's house, hollering his intentions to Gregor. The faintest hint of a thought process tinted the white emulsion of his words. He included 'stole the ballgame' and 'kill', ending his sentences with 'I sure will'. He was baffled at his recent injury. It felt like an invisible truck had piled into him, smashing his leg. Now he used his crutches to batter at Barny's door.

After the failure of the statue therapy, Doctor Perfect had advised Gregor to openly express his feelings to one and all, but Gregor was now bound into a network of ropes and pulleys he had rigged up to keep safe above the big cats. Edgy had warned him therapists were laughably out of touch with the exigencies of real life. Haggard and feverish, his clothes torn and a spider monkey on his face, Gregor looked across at the beaten body of Golden Sid, which hung lank in a snarl of ropes like a netted seal. 'Sid!' he hissed, trying to wake the man while not disturbing any more animals. The leopard prowled back and forth below, tormented with hunger. The snaggled stairwells and galleries were out of reach, spinning. 'Remember what Violaine said: "Sleep is but the—'

A loud hammering at the door woke both Sid and the lion, amid a caterwauling of dogs, chimps and exotic birds. A chameleon fell unnoticed from the wall. Sid began screaming, tears spitting from his eyes with the force of blowdarts.

'Sid,' Gregor snuffled through the monkey's belly, 'we can use the distraction. Get a swing going on the ropes, you can reach the window.'

A brown wave of chimps tumbled up the walls toward them, springing across and subjecting the two unfortunates to the worst kinds of inconvenience. One swiped Golden Sid's specs and placed them on its own face, springing away. Sid seemed equally bug-eyed without them. Gregor swung several times toward him, finally snagging his rope bundle and clinging on. 'Isn't it time you put all this behind you?' he hissed at the sobbing man. The door below splintered open, the subsequent commotion of pouncing predators and deadly injury disturbing a cloud of birds which swarmed upward at Gregor and Sid. 'I'm hit!' screamed Gregor – letting go of Sid, he swung in a wide arc toward the opposite window and exploded through it.

G.I. Bill slammed from the house, hobbling down the gangplank as the door banged again behind him, a big animal pounding close. He turned in time for the lion to swipe him hard upside the face. Then a leopard skittered fast across the lion's back and the two went into a rolling frenzy, blurring dust. G.I. Bill began dragging himself away from this turmoiling violence, and came face to face with a small spaniel, which bit him on the nose and then seemed to laugh. Getting to the phone box over the road, he drew the door closed and called Spacey's gas station. As he waited for someone to pick up, he watched the dog sitting sentry outside. It looked like it was wearing eyeshadow.

Five minutes later, Mike Abblatia arrived in a tow truck to find a lion and a leopard stalking the street. G.I. Bill leapt from a tree and landed on the truck roof, dragging Mike out and stealing the vehicle.

Erno set up the stepladder and gave the mike a few last minutes. The Mayor was telling the effigy tale again. In his many months as a whipped cur, Erno had heard it a dozen times.

'. . . Exhausted and panting, my eye alighted on a tiny red stone amid the ground's grit and gravel. Reaching down to pick it up, I found on closer examination that it was a microscopic effigy of myself, carved out of flint and painted dull red. At that moment I knew I'd grow up to become a fat overlord. And yes, here I am.'

'I've heard it a dozen times, Mayor,' sighed Max Gaffer.

'So regret me. I'm thrilled to bits, I must say.' The Mayor went on to the balcony and gripped the rail, breathing lustily and gazing out at the square. 'Even hell hounds look cute from up here. High balconies don't go around demanding action do they?'

'You're thinking about the Parade.'

'Looking forward to it, Max. Which is my best side, d'you think?'

Max Gaffer made a rambling, convoluted remark about the Mayor's Picasso morality, by which his morals were crowded on to one side of his face. 'But it doesn't matter,' he added. 'These voters and their wacko, ravaged heads are all for you.'

'I think you're right. With the powerhouse wonders of my cunning? So what if you and your echoing goons couldn't find Juno? He's about as fierce as a sardine. Now that he's served his purpose it's better for us he's out of the limelight. Keep them squared away.'

'When you fake a threat you grant options to trouble.'

The Mayor came in from the balcony. 'If needs be we'll sort him later. We've got a full roster of Parade float applications and your forms have gone down a treat. People despaired of the staggering cross-hatched career section. Understanding it's the work of ten men. I commend you.'

'Thank you sir. I laughed a lot.'

'And the new bond plan's a winner. Coin of the dark realm. It'll all work according to my inspiration.' The Mayor perched on the corner of his desk, chuffed and casual. 'Ah, Max, power's a funny thing. Thrombosis money and gamy combustion. A stranger blowing worms from his nose and saying we have his support. Forty pints of plasma always on hand. Thumbs touching brains without a diagram. Transport moving the bare necessities. Wrinkled mouths tearing at children. Flames wrecking the bales of hats. Hunchbacks ordering pizza. Bilge spurting out of necks. Bees fill the cake, wine jackets the senses, bird faces disintegrate against the darkness and drawling layabouts rattle at the handles. Laughter as my ashes blow back in your dry face. Summer days.'

'You lost me there Mayor, but thanks for sharing it anyway.'

The Mayor spotted a floor lobster which had appeared during his reminiscences. Frisky and playful, he picked it up in both hands and tossed it at Erno. 'Missed one, Erno,' he chortled.

Erno calmly climbed the stepladder and began removing the fan crossbar and hidden mike. During his labours Erno had come to three conclusions about revenge: it was humble in its toil, it aped more traditional hobbies, it was symmetrical when viewed over time. The recordings were his farewell message to servitude, the fart upon which he would jet into the sunset. He too was looking forward to Parade Day.

When Mike had been sitting in the tree for a while and the two big cats were nesting contentedly below him, he happened to look over at the ramshackle Juno house. Through an upper window, he saw a man braced in some kind of rope-and-pulley system. Above this, sitting on the roof, was the man they called the Round One, swinging his chubby legs back and forth like a kid's. The three men smiled and waved vaguely at each other, nodding.

Night was falling. The cicadas began to call.

Flickering his way around the wind, Dietrich folded himself and dropped through the night like a dead bird. Banging on to a rough backroad, he straightened up and shook the veined downpour of his head. Approaching on the road was a demon with da Vinci wings and eyes of broadband static. It strolled like an oldtime gentleman pacing his estate. Its head was a bladed mace which the demon had made a little effort to disguise with a torn woollen hood.

'Gettysburg, my brother in poison,' Dietrich announced. 'Mind if we walk and have a quick natter?'

'By all means,' said Gettysburg, unsurprised.

It was a strange night. They walked in silence for a while through the scent of apples, a warm southern breeze hissing the whiskered trees.

'How's Kermit?'

'Oh, that one. Apparently he's stuck in a pipe.'

'Good old Kermit. And Rakeman?'

'Top o' the line demons, every one.' Dietrich paused, uncertain. 'So what do you do? Sell Indian relics by the road?'

'I get by. With the blind man in the observatory. I'm an assistant. I get a bed over the street noise, held from the window by a length of floor.'

'He doesn't see a meat demon embedded with tin.'

'Sees whatever he wants. The root of an object isn't necessarily the part to watch, as I found to my cost once when a waiter belted me.'

'A man ought to corrupt his neighbours, at least.'

'I'm not a man.'

'Yeah well you chose to live as one. So a demon then – that should be worse shouldn't it? I can't help being appalled. You're feeding the mask.'

'Uh-huh. Well my conscience is as clean as an operating room, old friend.'

'Conscience. That's you, Getty. All right, dive into the waters of majority, see if you get clean.'

'Majority? You misunderstand everything. I have the precious gift of patience. Time means nothing to me.'

'That isn't patience. It's disregard.'

'You're wrong. I disregard only fashion.'

'So I see. Is that really a balaclava?'

'Yes. It's rented.'

'So this is what my master's up against,' Dietrich remarked dryly. 'A rented balaclava. Dare I tell him such fearful news.'

A warm rain began to fall. Gettysburg knelt and picked up a traumilus shell. 'So what's up?'

'Someone's thieved from His Majesty. Some meaty lizard that's absorbed a full load off the nets. Not human, just a snack. But etherically the thief's a bit tricky.'

'I saw the posters. He must have been angry when that

picture was taken. Propaganda's a poor union of gesture and delusion.'

'Nice. It's so simple-minded up here, isn't it? I find these 3-D buffoons such easy meat. The day's sworn and boring.'

'On the contrary, Dieter. I believe you find it chaotic beyond endurance. Politics. The impossibility of disgrace. You're a lightweight.'

'I can't feel compassion for flattened cats in the street like carpet samples.'

'You don't mean that remark. It's glued on.'

'With rusted blood I suppose.'

'Don't.'

'So the defection thing. What's the racket in putting your minutes here?'

'I learn stuff.'

'Example.'

'Well,' said Gettysburg thoughtfully. 'Light mixes with the wind. Gulls ride at personal risk. Dreams cling to criminal wombs. Nobody slips sitting. The direction of flatfish is impossible to anticipate. Honesty tastes bitterly of roses. A broken fountain blows aside a spray to blacken paths. Wounds open shockingly fast. When a man is unhappy, cupboards crowd him and cabs pass by. Likewise when a man is happy, cupboards crowd him and cabs pass by. Teeth and celery don't mix. Gardens lay dripping by the riverside. Rubies on a lean man are wasted. Memories, overweight, are the pits.'

'You've gone flesh-simple.'

Rain was swarming through the trees. Gettysburg breathed deep, his head glittering like a depth charge. 'This stuff's more interesting than cold treasure like the noble void, or your flames and dark wage. Dumb people cast an honest shadow, at least. Hooligan night's innocent in its old-fashioned simplicity – even within the plastic shell of celebration they've their own reasons for enjoyment. See for yourself in a few days. Everyone busts out in consolation and gum display. A parade – it might interest you.'

'Everyone?'

'Oh.' Remembering something, Gettysburg extruded a pocket of pullular skin from his flesh coat and retrieved something. 'I got those fags, by the way.' He proffered the cigarettes to Dietrich.

The hammerhead demon was distracted, ignoring the cigarettes. 'I'll see you Getty,' he said finally, and deployed his wings, ascending like a cannonball.

Three trucks stolen, marvelled Mike Abblatia. Ah well, forgive and forget.

The only one of the three men still awake, Mike saw the two big cats get suddenly spooked and dart away inside the dark house. His back was killing him. He was about to climb down when he saw two weird, giant guys standing near the tree, having a discussion and ignoring the rain. One had a head like a hammer, tubular hair which hung like soaked macaroni and a body of eroded armour. The other had a head like a spike glove and a ground-skimming coat of white leather. As he gestured, the spikehead's eyes flashed in the night like dashboard lights. They seemed to reach an impasse, and spike offered hammer a cigarette. Hammerhead unfurled a massive superstructure from his shoulders and flew upward, banging through the tree's furthest branches in a splat of leaves.

The spikehead seemed to think for a moment and then tapped out a cigarette for himself, lighting it by dabbing it into his eye. He stood there in the rain enjoying it, the blue smoke wraithing thin around him until, as Abblatia watched, he vanished as miraculous as a headache.

The spare bed was on the small granular shore of a subterranean sea. A jet black expanse of water was rippled by a breeze from the distant cave mouth, a low opening which showed a sliver of the night sky. Barny's bed was a few feet from the tide, the bedside table wedged against the grotto wall. He had fallen asleep counting bats in the dark ceiling, and when he roused an ambient light was wobbling around as though a shine of liquid and shadows were generated underwater. The slice of sky was lightening and the cavern had turned real marine, a pure green gold.

'Look simultaneously at the horizon and the detail in coins,' said Chloe Low, padding down from the passage. 'There's a test of perspective.'

'What's that – Violaine?' Barny asked, sitting up.

'No, it's father.'

'Where is he?'

'He's sat upstairs looking to his left. His tea genie's visiting. Come with me, I've got something to show you.'

'It's not a rotted turtle or something is it?'

She led him up the gradient of a tunnel panelled with polished oak. He watched her walk, wanting to thank every inch. They reached a level plateau. It was a gloomy hallway of cupboards and filigree. At one end was a painting with a bronze title plate set into the frame: *The sea is railed with teeth, the authority of nations*. Barny scrutinised the portrayal. Holes in the great swell of the ocean, yellow and blue boats in a havoc of water, passengers howling and moral, wearing bonnets. Chloe pulled at the painting and it swung outward like a cupboard door. On the rock wall behind it scrambled a phosphene blot of sickly light.

'Last time, you saw this from the other side,' she said, 'in the creepchannel. One time before that you wandered down here by accident and saw me coming out this side, and I had to bust you over the head with a drugged club so you wouldn't remember.' She looked at him and saw that he didn't get it. 'Okay, everything here has some kind of story or knowledge connected with it. The name of the game. But why not get the story direct? The creepchannel's one big etheric infection. It's tangled like spaghetti. In fact some of it actually is made of pasta. Like illness, it's a way of learning the worst.'

She showed him the soft underskin of her arm and drew a coaxial nerve cable from a pink scar.

'Once I'm in, I plug this into the creepchannel wall. I've seen stuff you wouldn't believe this way. Peacock fountain lands, copper gardenlocks of girls laughing, awe-white souls, temple hangings cradling the dead, stone banquets left in scatters. Voyages to invade swept away, golden victims, garment tides, unknown noble crews. Bitter military, rubble families, sweat and rumours, all that. And old stuff called snow, white ice floating down like dust. I sometimes bring objects back too.'

'Like Del's Fright Foundry.'

'He just reaches in and gets musty old ornaments. If you look at the Foundry from the other side, it's a storage closet.'

'Do you drive one of those creep cars, like Karloff Velocet?'

'I go to learn, not to travel. I have to be really touching all the stuff there.' She hid the hole behind the picture and hid her eyes behind her fringe. 'And it gets me off.' She sucked on the end of the nerve cable, fed it into her wound, and tugged down her sleeve. 'That's where I got the Violaine *Prophecies*, but I didn't tell father that. He needs things to be stumbled on, picked up at random, like the Kern gun. That's his prize exhibit.'

'I don't know who that is.'

They walked up the winding galleries toward the upper building. 'We're too young to remember. Kern was a hero, now he's dug under dirt and denial. Innovative resentment made him sample the moral fibre. What he discovered led him to build the gun and fire at the mayoral palace from the Tower of Nowt. They set the troops on him.'

'How'd he respond?'

'With some kind of capture, dying and funeral gambit.'

'Followed by a decomposition gambit?'

'Yes. He didn't die by the troops though. He was sentenced to death. While he was waiting for the bright hour he was attacked and killed by a flock of doves which fluttered through the barred window into his cell. They say he was the first Accomplice citizen to die that way. In his will he left the skeleton of a man wearing an iron cross, and a dog which barked when the weather was humid. I wish I could have met him.'

'Where have you put Mister Newton?'

'Your 'gator's comfortable, upstairs. Listen, father thinks

we can find an exhibit which'll help you with your problem. Take a gander at this.' She went into a storage room and sat next to a tea chest full of snot dust. 'There's a load of objects packed in here. Lucky dip.'

Barny rummaged and fished out a jewel-encrusted dog collar. Chloe took it from him. 'Okay. The collar belonged to Harley Quinn the architect. This guy built tower blocks out of dessert sponge so they'd dissolve before anyone could complain. He'd deny everything. The only person who didn't complain was Nana Rem, a designer in his office, who was in love with him. Her father owned the *Blank Stare* newspaper and hated Harley. Harley's was a delicate livelihood but the artwank crowd admired him, their appointment books squabbling like sparrows. A part of his head had been praised and relaxation became a real threat. He started trying to impress – forgot the mischief. Inspired by the night train, he built the ultimate council block – made of solid concrete, wall to wall, no doors or windows, no gaps inside for people to inhabit. Just a huge solid block. Nana's father helped in the construction of a by-the-numbers social outcry, fine lady swoon-progress halted by a chair and so on. Harley caught a fever and bagged a delirium vision of the world's crimes. These he plastered on to the outer wall of a gigantic dome and slated them over. Invited people to inspect the names under the tiles, but the public are so timorous Barny. They really believe in that one in a million chance: what if they peeled one up to reveal themselves? The dome was blown to pieces by the Mayor's office and Harley crashed with it. Rumour coils stiffened around him. Under stony scholars he kept mum, his face packed with people. Finally he tried ducking out to get his priorities, but Nana's father wouldn't leave him alone. Harley went to the local shaman – the old one, before Beltane Carom – who advised him to store his soul in plain sight. Harley chose one of a thousand Dalmatians in a dog pound, and the shaman installed him.'

'Dogs get everywhere,' Barny remarked pensively.

'Yes they do. So rumours of a soul procedure abounded but Nana Rem didn't know where he'd gone, and grieved. Nana's father followed up a joke story about a Dalmatian which had a blob on its coat in the exact shape of Harley's face, convinced that this was Harley himself. He bought the dog and used it as a mascot for the paper, mistreating it on the sly. In fact the dog, which finally sprang up and bit a hole in his face, was the wrong one. Nana could sense as much and went to the pound, finding the real Harley and bringing him home. She bought him this jewelled collar, and he lived the rest of his life happily, as her dog.'

'As her dog,' repeated Barny in a trance. Then he shook himself. 'How the hell does any of this legendary shit help me?'

'Give yourself up to the heavy machine of interpretation. It's the best way of hiding. Let's go see the 'gator.'

They went up, entering the round master bedroom. It was the cosiest chamber in the lamp tower. In a kingsize bed lay the reptile, wearing a frilly bonnet.

14

The Plunder Parade

Politeness lasts like a flower, then curls,
darkens and returns to itself

Mayor Rudloe ceremoniously donned his garland of tumours. 'We are scheduled to jubilate, Mr Gaffer.'

He cast open the balcony doors and stepped out. The crowd below was an irritating dissonance, a sea floating with trash. The Mayor bellied up to the microphone and began his address. 'It is with a heavy heart that I gaze upon your slack faces, upturned and vacant as ever. I've done precious little on your behalf while in office, except to receive the red levy and designate guilts to you all. I feel it the greatest honour to ease myself upon your industry. But someone asked me a question the other day, as I walked the streets of our community like a normal man. He was a citizen with bloodshot eyes and duds off a lorry. And his question was this: "Does the human muscular system differ from that of other creatures." Let me place your minds, such as they are, at rest. Muscle fibres differ from species to species of animal and also between parts of the same animal. There's the distinction between voluntary and involuntary muscles, and in structure and activity between striated muscle and smooth muscle. It seems basically that there's a great deal of variation on every level. So let us not pretend that all is ideal and pleasant. We have a bad statue problem in this town. The Steinway Spiders are of no small consequence. And we all know that the swamps are a hotbed of horseshoe crabs and illegal brain farming. I pledge to do whatever it takes to scour your inky hearts of desire. Bring me your huddled masses and I'll adopt a look of fierce consideration.

'But do not let alarm roast us black. Some say Accomplice is blocked in – I say it's cherished within walls of wonder. The baffling ocean to the south, the skeleton coast to the west, endless swampland to the east, and to the north a deadly chasm with a stumped, mined flyover. If those aren't tourist attractions I ask you what is. And when the rest of the world chooses to contact us, we'll be waiting for them, limbs akimbo. This pretence at a symphony of purpose is a real black eye for the scoffers. Vibrant buffoons unite!

'I, Mayor Rudloe, safekeeper of the Dung Signal and witness to the moral fibre, raise a momentary choice prayer to enterprise, and inform you at this time that there exists a golden opportunity for every man jack of you. I can suspend and relax my lower jaw by mental determination, at any time. The upper jaw is completely fixed. But it doesn't have to move for the purposes I have in mind. A brief demonstration.'

And Rudloe silently moved his lower jaw up and down like a ventriloquist's dummy.

'That's just a sample. Don't want to give too much away at this stage of the game, eh? The point is it has a thousand and one applications. I can begin marketing in two years with the right kind of backing early on. And that's where you come in. If each and every citizen purchases twenty registered jaw bonds, stamped and authorised, then beautiful in progress we will journey toward tether's end.

'So buck up. We are claiming this festivity is more precious than it is – which lights up our eyes with love. When all the while it's as good as stealing from you. Light up with simplicity, all! Inhale from flasks! Move many limbs at once! Madness onrushing! We celebrate!'

The torpid sermon would enjoy fame as a sedative. But now it was time to hear from doomed Eddie Gallo. As was traditional on Parade Day, the opposition mayoral candidate gave his speech sandwiched within a giant hamburger made of toughened steel and razor wire. Only his head hung free –

thankfully, perhaps, since he was naked. His new slogan was 'Badgers Can't Decide'. It was months before anyone discovered what it had meant – something to do with them having both black and white stripes. 'They also change directions sometimes when shuffling around,' he would explain later still. 'For that they have my sympathy.'

But today this was still obscure. In all innocence he'd bought a philosophy meant only for display. This was one of his few opportunities to display it. Level with the faces of the crowd, he was strained but cheerful. 'Hello. The day's quite hot, isn't it? Um, gravity – I'm thinking aloud here – gravity rearranges certain things. I have no reason to doubt that melting scarcely makes any difference, really. Who is to say we may not perform some easy operations drunken. Or in the blue gem jelly of sedative sleep. Running killer bee farms is a thing I never tried, because I heard it was too much like hard work. Bees are all sentiment, aren't they?'

Grimacing slightly as he shifted within his limits, he settled down again, breathing heavily.

'To the words of our Mayor – to that I say, the hands for his arms are held by bone, and with him as with everyone, er, well, shovel the wrong way and spuds – spuds resist. Melons are noses, visiting Eden – bulge, bulge – and grinning inside. I'm bewildered, d'you think that'll count against me? The same situation happens during negotiation. Well. A plank is a possession. Be happy. Let's hear no chit-chat about—'

'That's just grand,' the Mayor interrupted, applauding crisply, flushed with spite and good spirits. 'He had a great deal to say, didn't he. And now this year's appointed poet, with an airy thought for us all.'

Amy Gort stood on a scaffold podium in the square and leaned to the mike. 'Here's a poem called "My boyfriend claims his balls fly away at night".'

Scholar, gunner, cresting accuser
lost flock of birds
all this
in my fucking face

Alarmed, the Mayor frantically blustered into his microphone: 'Time to spit on your hands and take up the axe of jollity, everyone – let the Parade begin!'

The yearly Plunder Parade was held in honour of the thief Zeuxis Dyabell, who stole everything in the universe and, when hunted down by the mob and told to empty his pockets, turfed out every object imaginable. This creation myth was celebrated with floats bearing whatever the celebrants chose. The arbitrariness of the tradition resulted in some of the most hair-raising spectacles in the Accomplice calendar. As the crowd fused into emergency colours and the floats set off around the town, all was garish, ranging right across the visible spectrum of cackhanded trash. The gigantic shattered overcoat moved like nothing on earth, pumping stains into the air. A chipped life gallows shouldered along in glacial inevitability. A disembodied belly bulged down the street, dripping semolina and cod oil. Here rolled an open tank of dank water in which a non-swimmer perched yelling on a quivering quadbike. Waving to the crowd, King Verbal stood on a metamorphosing float of skeletal chaos, crystalline calcium exerting in all directions. A vicious knife fight occurred on a kind of wheeled raft, all seven combatants yelling continually that this should not be construed as endorsing the concept of violence. A man dressed as a hen stood on a frail float of woefully thin ham. Pulpy gourds and melons hung from a comical Steinway replica painted all the colours of the dead and studded with arrows. Doctor Perfect sat upon a giant rolling throne, crowned with his own rotted brain. Professionals giving a silent demonstration of 'deciding' began to convulse, dark spew fanning from their mouths. Microlady danced upon a hypodermic needle, her rolling platform fronted by a surgical magnifying screen. Fang rode smiling upon a painted wagon, his head running like a candy apple, and cast strips of his own flesh into the crowd. Like every other year, Dot Spacey juddered head first upon a titanic petrol cap. The master chef Quandia Lucent sat high in a saddle lashed to a giant pasta shell which trolled down the street like an anaemic beetle. Mimes lay completely immobile in a large wheeled deathbed. Magenta Blaze rode spreadeagled and gleeful on a rocket-sized tube of lipstick. One-day avatars flared into bonfires. G.I. Bill had fitted tank-tracks to a toilet and rumbled forward on this, waving a piece of radish and shouting something inaudible above the applause – what he had in mind was anyone's guess. An unmanned transparent inflatable blob was later said by Mr Peterson to be 'one o' them floating waterbugs o' the eye'. Biophantine butchers acted wooden scenes from Accomplice history on a float of laminated confidence. Dressed in doublet and hose they portrayed the tortuously mannered meeting of Bingo Violaine and the Clown of the North.

'How long has this handbag existed.'

'Precisely ten hours.'

'The man who made it was an expert.'

'Make your report that dignified always and we shall proceed well.'

Many in the crowd would later claim they had seen a cheerful Mike Abblatia hovering seated above the ground, his float having been stolen.

And amid and around it all were prancing processions of bloodsoaked waiters in boneseed masks which grew by the second, pushing out crests and antlers. Bastards on stilts tangled with mooring lines, toppling slow and beautiful, cloaks flowing. Farmers strode tricked out in clothes made of stained clay, bulrush antennae clashing together. A classic pagan green man went pale and started banging his heart with his fist. Twenty-three weeping sportsmen hugged each other, confessing their love. Inexplicable tableaux were enacted left, right and centre.

Edgy carried out the plan to advertise his book by padlocking himself into a trundling mobile cage with a dozen dogs. These animals had become instantly affronted at their captivity and took it out in snarling rage, biting the hell out of Edgy and each other in a whirling display of savagery. Edgy had prepared a banner detailing the book and its contents but at the last minute the title was changed to *I am a Failure*, and Edgy had frantically replaced the banner with this phrase scrawled on a piece of timber. There was nothing to indicate that this screaming, bloody, wretched captive was advertising an upcoming book.

After several days spent fending off a puma with a pair of nasal clippers Gregor stood utterly silent on a bare float, his clothes and flesh torn and patched with alley garbage. His face was blackened and swollen. In the crowd the Captain shook his head, disappointed.

The Mayor was represented by a massive silent replica of his own head, the lower jaw moving slowly up and down like a visor. Inside at the wheel, Erno geared up for his mighty moment.

B.B. Henrietta glanced as they entered the upper chamber and saw two pegs on a pedestal, between which was spread a strip of clinically pink meat. But she wasn't interested in the moral fibre. She went to the window, peering down at the passing procession.

'The life of a window includes the horizon and the wall,' rumbled Murdster the Sentinel, tending to arcane controls on the pedestal's fender.

'They certainly do,' muttered B.B. 'I mean, it does.'

The floats passed, crass and methodical. There was a deep pan pizza, a blacktie pike, a tubeless sports tyre. Once again the Church of Automata had snubbed the proceedings, while the Powderhouse was represented by a living pyramid of damaged personalities.

'The rain put moss in this house,' declared Murdster behind her, 'things began to get lumpy. I allow myself so few visitors here. I'm innocent of all delights but one.'

'Well now that shouldn't be,' said B.B. in a distracted way, then piped up, 'Hey Mr Murdster sir, do you know there's some sort of carnival or celebration going on down there? I had no idea – how lucky to be up here and get such a great view.'

'The Parade. It has a funerary grace.'

'Does it ever.'

'I anticipate all the more the peace concussion.'

'Oh I agree. I agree.'

Passing below was a red velvet float upon which a fierce-looking devil was guarded by a scruffy woollen ape with a pitchfork.

'Tradition is barbaric and formidable. Notions spoken on a rail. Bold music and toy voices. Flags like slabs. Empty-handed jesters bulwark our eyes against the circle of father death.'

'Sounds like a plan.'

'I am a repairman surrounded by jokes,' said Murdster, his voice thick and glutinous. 'My rusted truculence clattering about this belltower. Scraping a situation only makes the surface messy. But I'll shut the window on the holocaust of leaves. We gatecrash the fates together. Come, Bargain Basement Henrietta – I'll make you admit an unattractive virtue.'

'Eh?' B.B. turned around and first emitted a caw of laughter, then understood what she was seeing. Murdster, his face ghastly as a walnut, neck thorns flushed to bud with his exertions, was bent to the moral fibre and licking it with a tongue which resembled a hen's liver. Sweat glistened his corrugated forehead. He straightened up, ravening and a-shudder as he glared at her, his face congested with lust. B.B. volleyed a scream, the horizon spinning.

Dressed as an ape, Barny stood attendance beside the 'gator. It had been a simple matter to tog it up as the devil. Propped upright with scaffolding, garbed in red mask and horns, concealed wheels and a scarlet cape, it was a marvel of camouflage. The cherry on the cake was the use of Sweeney's salvaged teeth to hide the reptile's own. 'All I lack now is a sandwich,' thought Barny, wheezing with laughter.

Right about then B.B. Henrietta flopped out of an upper window in the Tower of Nowt, hanging rag-limp over the sill. This seemed to disturb the 'gator – it heaved a sudden thrash. Barny was caught between concern for B.B. and the stirring carnivore and yelled for help, pointing up at the Tower. The 'gator pumped its legs frantically, scooting off the float and into the crowd. Upright and with cloak aflow, it sped through them on its hidden wheels, teeth snapping. Many of the spectators felt their strongest emotion of the day. Once assured they were alive and intact after the evil one's passing, the onlookers turned to its hairy cohort with gobs of outrage.

Barny immediately opted for a basic running and panting gambit.

With the Parade well under way, Erno threw the switch. As the jaw on the massive mayoral head continued to move ponderously up and down, the Mayor's voice began to echo out: 'Offer a reward which we won't give. People despaired of the staggering cross-hatched career section. A stranger blowing worms from his nose and saying we have his support. The new bond plan's coin of the dark realm. People frying eggs on their cars *all* goddamn day. Laughter as my ashes blow back in your dry face.' Giggling like a kid, Erno peered out through the mouth to see the effect his work was having on the crowd, only to find that the crowd was gone, a last few spectators rushing off to the left.

Erno ejected himself from an ear of the mobile head as it motored along. Other floats had been abandoned askew or left to trundle through fences. There was something going on in the area of the square. Seething with baffled frustration, he stalked off in that direction.

The Captain hopped up on to Gregor's spartan float. His expression was clenched and grim. 'Gregor, I gave you a chance – I distinctly remember it – regarding your rambunctious public conduct. I even recommended medical assistance. And yet here I find you've rejected every social custom after all. Look around you – by golly man you've ruined the Parade.'

Gregor turned slightly toward him, his eyes bloodshot. It was not clear that he perceived the Captain at all. Certainly he offered no apology for his poor condition.

'Well?' the Captain demanded, embarrassed. 'For all that's sustainable, man, are you determined to stand there like a statue?'

Gregor's face seemed to crack with some extremity of grief, and he fell limply backward from the float as some commotion exploded past. When the Captain looked, he saw Gregor riding upon the back of the devil himself, pursued by an ape and a turbulent, screaming populace.

Perched on the Tower roof, Dietrich watched the crowd. Prearranged vigorous antics forgotten, they were entirely occupied with baying and stepping ever forwards. Despite all the excitement he saw faces not aglow with mischief but sealed closed as though with plastic glue. Were these the cheeky funsters Gettysburg admired? They wanted a way to express their resentment, not some theoretical joy. And they just got it. Barny, holding a fake pitchfork, caught up with his pig servant and gave it a few inaudible orders, then grabbed the disguised reptile by the cloak and guided it toward the mayoral palace.

Dietrich stood and fanned his wings. As he prepared to launch off, a woman hanging half out of a Tower window awoke from a stupor, saw him and screamed, falling from the window into a passing tank of dank water in which a non-swimmer perched yelling on a quivering quadbike.

An angled tumble of roofs and he was in the Mayor's office, shuttering his wings and examining the decor anew. The non-pliant pictures on the wall were indicative of a cornered philosophy. The Mayor, smoking a cigar, stirred bewildered, blinking at the intruder and wondering at his sudden entrance. One curtain flapped like a fish.

'Yer nemesis is at the door.'

'Eh now? What's this?'

'Barny Juno comes to barter and bargain. He has with him his pig servant and an alligator dressed as the devil. Bored dupes pursue him.'

The Mayor stood. 'You were here before. Representing yourself as some sort of man. Thought you'd swing by and stick your distorted oar in again eh? Max!'

'You'll want to give an enemy to the people, but I'll take the small matter of Juno and the reptile off your hands.'

'That creature's highly valuable,' the Mayor stated tersely.

'Oh? Where did you catch that idea?'

'A little birdy told me. A birdy with no neck, thick arms and a gillball shirt.'

Dietrich frowned. 'You're sure this was a *birdy*?'

Max Gaffer entered and stopped short, looking at the demon. The Mayor chucked an alert look at him. 'Throats to the wall, Max.'

A marble staircase echoed. An ape and the shambling, worse-for-wear pig servant entered, panting, followed by the 'gator, which thrashed in on all fours, caped but with its supports trailing. It opened its mouth in a long silent display of fangdom, finally slapping it closed and looking enigmatic. Barny tore off his gorilla mask, gasping for air.

Dietrich looked into Juno with his demon eyes. While the others here were matted with spiny rotwork and muddy toxins, and the Mayor was even now extruding another floor lobster through a tangle of etheric bile cables, Barny was a mere scaffold of running bone and nerve fire. He was a man entirely without suspicion. It was like looking at the simplest of animals. Love attached him to the 'gator like rich filamentous bunting.

'People are chasing us,' Barny cried. 'Help us, Mister Mayor.'

15

Death to Whoever

We may change; we may change a victim

The Mayor browsed lies before replying. Mouthing outside were the outraged; time to climb into a skip and make the best of it? The anvil-headed demon, all sneer ducts and mantis joinery, grinned wickedly. The minutes themselves would answer if the Mayor left it much longer. The century flower of his conscience still a tightfisted bud, he opted for a volley of offended bluster. 'I remain calm in the face of all provocation. But this goes beyond my visual register. Shelter? Protection? The head of a man and the body of an ape? A fork in one hand and set of false teeth in the other? Bringing your pig servant here? And that reptile, in a cape and horns? What . . . what's . . . ? Do you comprehend that this monster and its blunt snout and thrashing motions are completely lethal and I've been damn near growing tusks trying to tell everyone about it?'

'Mister Newton wanted to—'

'Who?'

'See the Parade. The 'gator.'

'Did you bar the door?'

'Of course.'

'It'll take them a good ten minutes to get through. Where's Erno? Look at these bloody floor lobsters. It's demolition of duty. Let him arrive on a stretcher or not at all.'

'Change of subject, Mayor?' asked the demon sardonically.

'Nothing of the sort. Er, Max, how's your underwear doing?'

'Eh?'

'I made an offer, Mayor,' the demon remarked, leaning slack and casual against a bookcase. 'My master. I can see him now, tearing brain from brainpan like a jellyfish from a rock. Your nose is a meal in itself.'

The Mayor swanned it, smooth and groundless. 'With respect, Mr Hammer or whatever your name is, I'm reluctant to get into further dealings with demons. Remember that Adopt a Horned One campaign a few years ago, Max? Punishing paperwork. Black and yellow ectoplasm on the chairs. Treating the floor lobsters like kittens. God help us.' The scheme had been popular among the well-to-do and a formal signing ceremony had taken place. Upon signature a dozen shrill, spicy freaks actually showed up. These crimson slurry princes made short work of their patrons, closing serrated jaws on heads and bursting eyes like berries. The Mayor had had to dispose of eight bodies by fire. He turned quickly to Barny. 'Here's the bottom line, Juno – what do you want?'

'Well, I could use a fully-antlered adult caribou if you've got one.'

The Mayor sighed with grievous disappointment, glanced at the demon and slowly drew himself up, to mutter with salvaged pride: 'Very well sir. Certainly, come over and intervene, by all means.' He gave Barny a look of distaste. 'We're all friends here.'

'Then here's my suggestion,' stated the demon. 'Dress some convenient lackey in that cape and devilwear. Chase him out on the balcony with the pitchfork and pretend to thwart him in the glare of the public. They're morons to a man, heads searing with detergent. This is politics. Words of certainty alter their course. Death cools the blood.'

The Mayor gave an urgent hiss. 'Max? The smart move?'

'Yes, stage a valiant exploit,' nodded Max Gaffer thoughtfully. 'Outstanding.'

'Good, then let's tog up the pig servant,' announced the Mayor.

Gregor roused very slightly.

'Gregor,' Barny whispered. 'They want to dress you like the devil.'

'It was only a matter of time,' he sighed with a smile.

At that moment Erno entered, panting.

'Erno – thank god for the servants' entrance. He'll make a better evil one, eh?'

Erno stopped, looking at the assembled figures. Worry hung on the wall above his head. Max plucked the cape and horned eye-mask from the 'gator and danced up to Erno, throwing the cape across his shoulders. The Mayor took the pitchfork from Barny.

'You'll serve, my quiet boy,' the Mayor chuckled. He swerved the stunned, gaping Erno toward the balcony door, and paused. 'I hear popular panic, and I love it.' Then he strode out, pushing Erno ahead of him.

The crowd roared when they saw the horned demon backing on to the balcony. 'You've the strutting arrogance to interfere with our bucolic celebration, eh horn boy?' the Mayor bugled, sweeping into view. 'You and your Aztec nostrils. Yes, you. I'm not making this up. I'm ruddy furious and here's the visual proof.'

He struck forward with the pitchfork and Erno grasped the shaft – a precarious tussle ensued. 'Help,' Erno said wanly, but nobody heard him.

'Repulsive oversight, bump to a halt here,' proclaimed the Mayor and shoved forward with the fork. Tipping over the rail, Erno fell with a dismal bleat, landing on the poetry platform with his mask askew.

The cloak hung snagged on the balcony rail. Mayor Rudloe sensed the grind-stoppage of synapses amid the onlookers. Erno was recognised. Conversation stirred.

A face poked through the curtains. 'They think you planned the entire thing,' said Max Gaffer in a husky whisper. 'Make light of the situation.'.

'Doesn't matter,' the Mayor called out, shrilly casual. 'Power's purified by the death of small fry. Yes, good old Erno – we all knew him. A real fighter, that one. Sixty of his mouth screams slammed up at his attacker. The landlord of life has draped the towel on his pump. And I love you all.'

All I need now, thought the Mayor, is a heart attack or seizure. The sympathy would come pouring down as though from a tipped vat.

But before anything of the kind could occur, the mayoral float burst through a fence and trundled across the square, its jaw working slowly, projecting the Mayor's voice: 'You can't go wrong spending money on death and murder. Lucky for men like me. However far we ascend in office, we never reach those heights where the law dwells. Phrase horrors like an invitation and you'll get a crowd. Shake my hand, Max. I'm a bastard. I'll insult everyone necessary and do little else for now. Juno – do you understand that I'm basing my campaign on a demonisation of you and your supposed depravities? I rue the fates for making me mayor of a place so obscure it's where ants go to die. I'll break you, Erno.'

The giant artificial head was making its way toward the palace through the parting populace.

'That's . . . not my voice,' shrieked the Mayor. 'I loved that man.' He pointed down at Erno's body. 'He was like a son to me.'

The giant head crashed to a halt against the poetry lectern, its jaws opening and closing on Erno's body while booming the words: 'That'll put fish in his custard. Erno, you silent bastard. I knew I'd grow up to become a fat overlord. All we need is deceit, an enemy, and negligence. Shake my hand, Max. There's nothing to stop us.'

'I'll never understand political strategy,' said doomed Eddie Gallo from his steel encasement.

'All right!' yelled the Mayor with scornful superiority. 'I admit my heart's a howling wasteland! Thrive you all in misgivings and misery! Cretinous wretches! Credulous bloaters! You'll even vote for me yet! Damn you all!' And he threw himself inside as the crowd erupted.

'Way to go, sir,' said Max Gaffer archly, stuffing a few necessaries into a bag. 'Fires will bond this moment to our memory.'

The demon gave a sharp laugh. 'It's the starving dog that leads us to the body,' he said, speaking unfolded and triumphant at last. His leather wings batted open, darkening the room. 'Time to see the blade sever the looking-glass, Juno. We're leaving. I'll go easy on the animal if you come along quietly.' And he raised an open claw toward Barny.

Throughout the above events Barny had been wondering about the reptile's health. It was really too big for Mister Spiderman's old terrarium and all this excitement was disturbing. He wondered if he should release it in the swamp. His father was always saying there was nothing very fierce or challenging out there.

So when the weird guy reached out and said he'd get them out of here, he automatically grasped the claw, forgetting he was holding Sweeney's jaws in that hand. Then the demon was screaming, black liquid spurting from a stumped wrist – his claw lay on the carpet. Two floor lobsters began to show interest in it.

'And there's your answer,' came a voice from behind him, and there was a tall guy looking more dead than he had a right to, shrinking his wings. He had flickering eyes the colour of nothing and wore a white vinyl coat. 'What was your method, Dietrich? Sneer to establish teeth, cast a sharp shadow, angle your noggin? And bloodshot eyes – that's the cardinal rule. Don't you get bored with it all?'

'You're another demon,' snapped the panicked Mayor, rifling his desk drawers for a weapon. 'Think you're fooling anyone with that derby hat?'

'No? Well, I had a balaclava but it was only rented. I had to return it.' The pale demon removed the hat, revealing a skull like a bladed mace. 'Mr Rudloe – we've never met exactly. Gettysburg's the name. The people will be in this room in two minutes. Some will clobber you with fragments of timber. Others will drag you down the stairs by the right leg. Whether any of this will effect your votes, what do you reckon. They demand only satisfaction. Nice flowers in that vase, by the way.'

'Getty,' snarled Dietrich. 'This is entrapment.'

'You think I'll accept a thing just because some wag of a demon drew my attention to it?' the Mayor shouted. 'Max, these wingnuts think I give a damn.'

'You speak on the dotted line, Mr Rudloe,' said Gettysburg, a beehive behind his eyes. 'And your man there's full of dust and chilled tar.'

'Saying this sort of thing to them's like throwing a carpet under a bird,' gasped Dietrich, bent over his cradled arm. 'Like it matters.'

'It does matter,' said Gettysburg. 'I live here.'

'Accomplice's little trophy demon.'

'So regret me.'

Behind Gettysburg a crimson stain bloomed quickly on the door, bulging into meat which made the doorway an oblong clot. A gap flumed open at the centre, fast cold air flying from it.

'Barny Juno. I know a shortcut. The four of us are leaving.' Gettysburg patted Gregor on the head, took his hand and walked toward the gore door, looking to Barny to follow. Barny led the 'gator through the block of meat and a gush of bloodwater swept the room away.

Dietrich threw himself after them.

16

Going Through Hell

Never arrive at a funeral by parachute

Nothing in Gregor's career as a coward had prepared him for the events in that room. The two towering demons had made everyone else children. Now he seemed to be roving the byways of reason. Looking back, he saw the Mayor's office rocketing away, its final circumstances branded on to his retina. Seconds after the demon Gettysburg dragged them through the gore door, the enraged citizenry seemed to have burst through the underlying one, so that they appeared to be trampling away from this hellish tunnel. Dietrich had thrown himself forward and G.I. Bill, tripping on a gathering of floor lobsters, barrelled into him, embedding his solid head in the demon's stomach. The Mayor and his lawyer were set upon by the cacophonous masses. 'Don't touch the underwear!' screamed Max.

'Your underwear is not the matter at hand!' the Mayor managed to thunder. Three children made a spirited attack upon his leg and began to drag him away. The Mayor attempted to bargain. 'My leg maintains that it must live in my house!'

And then Gregor looked ahead, rushing weirdness hammering past him. It was a ride through schemes, the blurwalls ringing with scionic squeals.

Then they were stood on a companionway over horror, Gettysburg pointing like a tourist. Deep detail in big time. Structures infinite. Tortured miles flavoured with accidents.

'Mere corpses don't make them proud. Oak can mature about a body. Nothingness is a waltz, vacuums twitching.' They were coasting past galaxies of criticism and society, black breath blasting through them. Body fat was cooked into tears. 'Apocalypse. Stink millions swelling and throwing sparks.' A billion migrating dunces crossed a chaos of unvoiced assumptions. 'Dark matter sometimes breeds in silence. Children here meet the floor without mattering, lost magnificently in nursery forges.' Bladeshadow shivers of locusts turned heads in regard, piling hivesights into roofs, mandibles frozen in mealstab. 'Revenant market. Head trauma unit. Sweeney's torturers. They're obsessed with beauty.' A couple of poor fiends attempted to eat fruit in difficult circumstances.

Gettysburg made his three charges peek out of a vent in the sickstone wall of a cavern, looking miles down at a parasite the size of a horse. The white arachnoid was braced at the bullseye of an etheric nerve sea, electricity exploding between the cables. 'Sweeney.'

Bubblewrapped in Gettysburg's protection, they drifted along a narrow ledge. 'You'll like this.' Below were a load of ruins piled in a corner. 'Violaine *Prophecies*.' He pointed at some blather engraved on a sulphate slab:

> Beware the Beast Man, simple and true.
> He'll kick the living shit out of you.

Gettysburg elbowed Barny, wounding him badly. 'Who could that be eh, Juno?'

They were moving through darkness, walking now. Dim clutter and junk were stacked here. Gregor read off labels. 'Skull sandpaper. Mole pearls. Umbilia.'

All but the demon were shivering, frozen. They pushed through a door into another collection of lethal novelties. Looking to the left, Gregor saw a rigid goat standing behind a counter. They were in the Shop of a Thousand Spiders. Night had fallen. Gregor remembered the darkling creep exit at the rear of the store, then began almost at once to forget it.

Barny seemed more scared now than ever. Even the demon Gettysburg seemed suddenly cautious. Spooky Staring Boy was somewhere on the premises.

They crept toward the door, jumpy and almost free. Gregor just wanted to be sleeping in his burrow under the office. The night looked fresh and healthy. Barny put his hand to the handle.

'The throat was shocked before lines cut little rubies,' said a voice behind them. They turned to see the small figure staring blandly at them. 'And the grave digests in plump welcome.'

Edgy lay in the Aquarium Hospital, his symptoms exposed to the world. In beds to either side of him lay Gregor and B.B. Henrietta. B.B. lay stiff as a plank, staring into the sky. The three spoke very little. Edgy was wrapped almost entirely in bandages and wished he was allowed to recuperate back at the motel – he could easily incorporate the look into his ghost scam.

Barny was visible a long way off, navigating the glass corridors. With him was the 'gator, loping its short legs forward with a slap. And finally here he was, beaming at the three. 'I brought grapes,' he said, dumping a bag on to a side table. The 'gator dragged its tail past a glass medical stand which crashed to the floor, bursting a plasma packet. 'And grubshoots. Guaranteed to dart up the walls and snap at any bugs around here, then rot to grey in the corners.'

'He brought the 'gator,' mumbled Gregor, and pulled the invisible covers over his head.

'Get that monster away from me,' shouted B.B., 'you *lunatic*!'

'It's perfectly legit,' said Barny.

'That's not the point, Bubba, oh tell him Edgy, tell him in a way he'll understand!'

The Captain entered, dapper as always in his white uniform. 'How's the staff?'

'Mine's worked better,' said Gregor.

'Before you say anything, ma'am,' Barny told the Captain,

'I've decided to say goodbye to Mister Newton here. People aren't good for him.'

'Well by golly in light of the traditional revelations about Mayor Rudloe at this time of year, I think I can set aside his allegations about you. And I just had a chat with Doctor Perfect – it seems I owe you an apology, Gregor. He says he advised you to hot-damn express your feelings directly to one and all and this you sensibly did. But I came here primarily to see Mr Plantin Edge.'

'Me. What have I done?'

'I witnessed your little display in the cage full of dogs. I must say I've never seen a more reckless and stupid act in my life.'

'Well listen,' groaned Edgy from a ragged hole in his bandages. 'Who's to say the dogs, at least, didn't enjoy it.'

'It was a mad, brash act, and on the strength of that I'd like to give you the glad hand and invite you to join the Patently Damaging Sports Club.'

'Eh? You?'

'Oh yes. I've been a member for some years. Threw myself arse-first into a barrel of rattlers. Rather amateur really – you'll learn, as I did.'

'But I've been trying to get myself invited by Neville Peth. He doesn't seem to think I'm worthy.'

'Neville Peth isn't in the club. He sells insurance, for pity's sake. And I'll tell you another thing.' The Captain turned and strode out.

'I wish he wouldn't do that,' said Gregor.

Sweeney sat in a pall of noxious steam. 'Look. I'm bonded again in this bloody network hull. I only sat down for a moment. There must be a better way of keeping a grip on things.'

Preoccupied with the rope darkness of his stomach, Dietrich did not reply. A mess of wing blood, ink and steel, he stumbled down the slope.

'Where's Juno? The 'gator? Dead at least?' Sweeney fidgeted in his throne, shrike cables flubbering slow around him. 'Even that Bingo bastard said regarding human character, to simplify is to insult, to kill is to simplify absolutely. Straightforward enough.'

'Not dead, Your Majesty. I suspect . . . the Prophecy—'

'What's that?' Sweeney pointed at Dietrich's right arm, which now terminated with a sort of bone mantrap.

'Your . . . old jaw, Your Majesty. Floor lobsters ate the claw. I had to use what I had. It's bloody chaos up there. Those . . . people. They're not civilised. Getty's insane to love them. Look at my stomach.'

Boiling with rage, Sweeney flushed the colour of black glass. 'Gettysburg? You've been consorting with that turncoat?'

Dietrich didn't know what to say.

'And no Juno? Get out of here!'

Dietrich turned and blundered away.

Sweeney stared about at the empty cavern. 'Dare I send anyone for cigarettes?'

And he wept chains which dangled clinking from his face, tenting the skin.

Barny took the 'gator to the swamp, releasing it into mile upon mile of twisting waterways and mangrove islands. Determined that the reptile should be forgotten, he took one of the creature's teeth and gave it to Chloe Low in the Juice Museum. Before filing it among the other exhibits she held it in her hand and closed her eyes. 'It says: "I bite for you, I chew for you, but taste nothing. Teeth are the citizens of the body." Hmm, it's like that sometimes. I'll put it with the gun, shall I?'

Then they sat on a rock by the baffling ocean and smelt the salt of the moon. Shadows ate the valley, dead men dappled in the morgue and the cold middle of a church got even colder.

But there's more.